The Organ Broker

The Doctor's Dilemma Collection, Volume 5

Dr. Nilesh Panchal

Published by DrMedHealth, 2024.

This is a work of fiction. Similarities to real people, places, or events are entirely coincidental.

THE ORGAN BROKER

First edition. October 25, 2024.

Copyright © 2024 Dr. Nilesh Panchal.

ISBN: 979-8224169351

Written by Dr. Nilesh Panchal.

Publisher Information

COPYRIGHT © 2024, **DrMedHealth**.

All rights reserved.

No part of this book may be reproduced, distributed, or transmitted in any form or by any means, including photocopying, recording, or other electronic or mechanical methods, without the prior written permission of the publisher, except in the case of brief quotations used for review purposes or academic references.

Under no circumstances will any blame or legal responsibility be held against the publisher, or author, for any damages, reparation, or monetary loss due to the information contained within this book, either directly or indirectly.

Before reading the book, please read the disclaimer.

For permissions, inquiries, or other correspondence:

drmedhealth.com@gmail.com

For more information, please visit.

www.DrMedHealth.com[1]

---

1. http://www.DrMedHealth.com

Disclaimer

THE CONTENT OF THIS book is a work of fiction. Names, characters, places, medical scenarios, and incidents are either the product of the author's imagination or are used fictitiously. Any resemblance to actual persons, living or dead, real-life medical events, organizations, or institutions is purely coincidental.

The medical procedures, treatments, and conditions described are for narrative purposes only and should not be interpreted as professional advice. Readers are advised not to use the medical information presented in this book as a substitute for consulting healthcare professionals or seeking proper medical care.

Neither the author, Dr. Nilesh Panchal, nor the publisher, **DrMedHealth**, assumes any responsibility for actions taken based on the information contained within these novels. Any opinions expressed in the book are solely those of the author and do not represent the views of any affiliated institutions or organizations.

Chapter 1: Heart of Darkness
Chapter 2: The First Cut
Chapter 3: Meeting the Broker
Chapter 4: Price Tag on Humanity
Chapter 5: Ghosts on the Operating Table
Chapter 6: Into the Underworld
Chapter 7: Blood Money
Chapter 8: The Anatomy of Betrayal
Chapter 9: A Knife to the Throat
Chapter 10: Fractured Oaths
Chapter 11: Shattered Masks
Chapter 12: Organ Farm
Chapter 13: Chasing Redemption
Chapter 14: The Scalpel's Edge
Chapter 15: The Final Trade
Chapter 16: After the Harvest

Chapter 1: Heart of Darkness

Dr. Arjun Malhotra had spent years mastering the intricacies of the human heart—its chambers, valves, electrical impulses, and vulnerabilities. He had saved countless lives, performed surgeries with precision, and earned the respect of his peers. But nothing in his extensive medical career had prepared him for the chilling words spoken in that sterile hospital room.

"We've done everything we can."

The cardiologist in front of him—a colleague, a friend—spoke gently, as if softer words could lessen the weight of the news. Arjun sat in stunned silence, his mind grasping for some kind of anchor. His wife, Meera, sat beside him, her hands gripping his so tightly it hurt.

"How long?" Arjun whispered, his throat tight with the question.

Dr. Kothari glanced down at his clipboard, clearly uncomfortable. "Six months... maybe less. An immediate transplant is the only chance, but the waitlist... it's not moving fast enough."

Arjun's heart raced, pounding in his ears like a drum. A strange numbness crawled up his spine, leaving him cold

THE ORGAN BROKER 5

despite the suffocating heat in the small room. His eight-year-old son, Aarav—his vibrant, curious boy who loved dinosaurs and building LEGO spaceships—was dying. A heart too weak, too flawed, was slowly betraying him from within.

Meera sobbed quietly, her shoulders trembling, but Arjun could do nothing but sit there, frozen. Every part of him wanted to scream, to tear apart the unfairness of it all, but he knew it wouldn't change a thing. Not unless he found a solution. A heart.

"The list..." Arjun began, struggling to keep his voice steady. "What if we—"

"We're doing everything we can," Kothari interrupted, already knowing where the conversation was headed. "There are hundreds of patients in similar situations. Children, adults... You know how this works, Arjun."

Yes, Arjun knew. Organs were scarce. The waitlists were governed by ethics and fairness, not by desperation or influence. Aarav's condition had worsened too quickly—there was no time to wait for some tragic accident to yield a donor match.

"There must be another way," Meera choked out, her eyes puffy and desperate.

Kothari shook his head slowly. "You know the protocols. I wish there were. But... I'm sorry."

The words landed like a death sentence, hollowing out whatever strength Arjun had left. Kothari squeezed his shoulder briefly before leaving, the door clicking shut behind him, leaving the couple alone with the suffocating silence of their grief.

Arjun drove home that evening in a daze. The city lights blurred into streaks of color through his windshield, but he barely noticed. Meera sat beside him, her hand resting limply in her lap, her gaze lost in some distant, unreachable place. Neither of them spoke during the long, painful drive. What was there to say?

When they arrived home, Aarav was asleep on the couch, his small chest rising and falling with an alarming fragility. His pale skin looked translucent under the dim glow of the living room lamp. Arjun knelt beside his son, brushing a curl of dark hair from his forehead. The sight of his boy—so full of life, yet hanging by a thread—nearly shattered him.

"How do we tell him?" Meera whispered behind him, her voice cracked from crying.

Arjun didn't answer. He didn't know how to explain to an eight-year-old that his heart might give out before he could grow up, that all the toys and dreams he had collected might never come to fruition. How did you tell your child he was running out of time?

The days that followed passed in a blur of hospital visits, specialist meetings, and sleepless nights. Aarav's condition worsened with alarming speed. Each time he coughed or clutched his chest in pain, Arjun felt the ground slipping away beneath him. They tried medications, oxygen therapy, even experimental treatments, but it was like trying to put out a wildfire with a bucket of water.

Then came the moment that would change everything.

Late one night, after another hospital visit, Arjun sat alone in his study, staring at the mountain of medical research on his desk. He had exhausted every official avenue—there was no loophole, no miracle treatment, no way to bypass the waitlist without a donor. Time was the only thing Aarav didn't have.

His phone buzzed, pulling him from his thoughts. It was an unknown number. Normally, he would have ignored it, but something made him pick it up.

"Dr. Malhotra," a deep voice on the other end said, smooth and deliberate. "I hear you need a heart."

Arjun sat up straight, his pulse quickening. "Who is this?"

"Someone who can help. But help comes at a price."

For a moment, Arjun thought it was some cruel scam—some opportunist preying on desperate parents. But there was something disturbingly genuine about the man's voice. The calmness, the certainty.

"Who are you?" Arjun repeated, gripping the phone tighter.

"They call me The Broker," the man said. "And I specialize in solutions when the system fails."

Arjun's heart pounded. "This is illegal."

"That depends on your definition of legality," the Broker replied smoothly. "The question isn't what's legal, Dr. Malhotra. The question is: how far are you willing to go for your son?"

The line went silent for a moment, as if giving Arjun time to process the weight of the question. He closed his eyes, the image of Aarav lying in that hospital bed flashing in his mind.

"How much?" Arjun whispered, the words slipping out before he could stop them.

"Meet me, and we'll discuss the details. Tomorrow. Midnight. I'll send you the location."

The line went dead.

The next twenty-four hours felt like a waking nightmare. Arjun paced the house, his mind spinning with fear and doubt. He knew what he was about to do was dangerous—insane, even. But as he watched Aarav struggle to breathe, gasping for air like a drowning child, all his moral reservations began to erode.

That night, as the clock neared midnight, Arjun kissed Meera goodbye, telling her he was going back to the hospital to check on some test results. It wasn't a lie exactly—but it wasn't the truth either. Meera gave him a weary nod, too exhausted to question him.

He slipped out into the cold night, his heart pounding as he drove toward the location the Broker had texted him earlier: an abandoned parking lot on the outskirts of the city.

When Arjun arrived, the lot was eerily empty, illuminated only by the dim, flickering glow of a streetlight. He parked his car and waited, anxiety twisting his stomach into knots.

A sleek black SUV pulled into the lot moments later, its headlights cutting through the darkness. The vehicle came to a smooth stop, and a tall, well-dressed man stepped out.

"You must be Dr. Malhotra," the man said with a smile that didn't reach his eyes. "I'm glad you came."

Arjun swallowed hard, stepping out of his car. "You're the Broker?"

The man nodded. "Let's not waste time. You need a heart. I can get you one. But it won't be cheap."

Arjun felt a cold sweat break out on his forehead. "How much?"

The Broker's smile widened slightly. "Not just money, Dr. Malhotra. We deal in favors, too. Surgical expertise, for

THE ORGAN BROKER 9

instance. You perform a procedure for us, and in return, we get your son what he needs."

Arjun's stomach churned. "What kind of procedure?"

"Nothing too complicated," the Broker said with a dismissive wave. "A transplant. For a... client of ours. Someone who can't exactly go through the regular channels."

Arjun's heart raced. He knew exactly what the Broker was asking. An illegal surgery, off the books, performed in secret. If he agreed, he would be crossing a line he could never come back from.

"And the heart for my son?" Arjun asked, his voice barely above a whisper.

"It'll be arranged," the Broker assured him. "A perfect match. Delivered within days."

Arjun felt dizzy, the weight of the decision pressing down on him like a crushing tide. He thought of Aarav—his bright eyes, his infectious laugh—and knew there was no other choice.

"Okay," Arjun whispered, sealing his fate. "I'll do it."

The Broker smiled, extending his hand. "Welcome to the dark side, Dr. Malhotra."

Arjun shook the man's hand, feeling as if he had just made a pact with the devil.

Chapter 2: The First Cut

The hospital was always bustling with a subdued, frantic energy—a place where time was measured in heartbeats, and every second could mean the difference between life and death. Dr. Arjun Malhotra moved through the halls with the same precision he had practiced for years, but now, each step felt heavier. His mind swirled with a grim cocktail of helplessness and guilt. Aarav's condition was deteriorating rapidly, and there was no donor heart in sight. Desperation gnawed at him like a persistent ache.

He arrived at the Pediatric Cardiology Ward, trying to push the heavy thoughts away. Routine. Focus on routine. It was the only thing that kept him from collapsing under the weight of his situation. He was scheduled to check on two post-op children today, both recovering from valve replacement surgeries. But as he rounded the corner, he noticed something unusual—an argument unfolding in one of the private rooms.

A woman's voice, sharp with anger and fear, echoed down the corridor.

"I don't care what you say. I need that liver! My son doesn't have time for your excuses!"

Arjun paused just outside the door, instinctively pulling back, though curiosity gripped him. Through the narrow window on the door, he could see a woman—mid-40s, well-dressed but disheveled—pleading with a doctor, her voice shaking. The boy lying on the bed beside her looked pale and skeletal, his face sunken, eyes too large for his gaunt frame. His chart pinned to the bed identified him as Sahil Rao, age nine. Liver failure. Terminal without a transplant.

The doctor she was arguing with—a junior resident—looked helpless, shuffling on his feet and repeating the same apologetic phrases Arjun had heard too many times in recent weeks.

"I understand, Mrs. Rao," the young doctor stammered, "but we can't jump the line. There are protocols, and the donor system—"

"Screw your system!" the woman hissed. "What good are protocols if they kill my son?"

Arjun lingered for a moment longer before stepping away, not wanting to intrude. But her words stayed with him, prickling his skin like needles. **What good are protocols if they kill my son?** He couldn't shake it. Wasn't that the same cruel truth he was grappling with? Aarav was slipping away because the system—however fair and ethical—was fundamentally flawed.

He forced himself to finish his rounds, but the image of Sahil's mother haunted him throughout the day. The desperation in her voice mirrored his own inner turmoil. What would a parent not do to save their child?

It was past midnight when Arjun finally left the hospital. Exhausted, he walked to the parking lot under the eerie hum of flickering streetlights. He unlocked his car and slid into the driver's seat, ready to head home to Meera and Aarav. But as he turned the ignition, a shadow appeared at his window, startling him.

It was Mrs. Rao.

She tapped on the glass, her face barely visible in the dim light. Arjun rolled down the window cautiously, frowning in confusion.

"Dr. Malhotra," she said in a hushed, urgent voice. "Do you have a minute?"

Arjun hesitated. "It's late—"

"Please," she cut him off, her voice cracking. "I just need a minute. It's about... options."

Something about the way she said it made his stomach twist. Options. He could hear the unspoken words between the lines—words that hinted at things no respectable doctor wanted to hear. Against his better judgment, Arjun nodded, unlocking the passenger door. She slipped inside the car, glancing around nervously before speaking.

"I know what you're going through," Mrs. Rao said quietly. "I've seen the way you look at your son. You're thinking the same thing I thought when Sahil's diagnosis came."

Arjun's pulse quickened. "What are you talking about?"

"I'm talking about the fact that the system is broken," she whispered, her eyes glassy with suppressed rage. "It's not fair. They tell you to wait, to hope, but they never tell you how to survive the waiting. They don't tell you what to do when hope runs out."

Arjun clenched the steering wheel, staring straight ahead. "What are you suggesting?"

THE ORGAN BROKER 13

Mrs. Rao leaned in closer, her voice dropping to a conspiratorial whisper. "There are ways, Dr. Malhotra. People you can talk to. They can get what you need. Quickly. No waiting lists, no bureaucratic bullshit."

Arjun's breath hitched. "You're talking about... the black market?"

She nodded, her expression hard and defiant. "Yes. And before you judge me, think about this—what's more important to you: following the rules or saving your son's life?"

Arjun felt the air leave his lungs in a slow, heavy exhale. "And how exactly does it work?"

"There are brokers," Mrs. Rao explained, her hands fidgeting in her lap. "They're connected to... people. Sources. It's expensive, and you'll need to do favors—surgical favors sometimes. But they deliver. They find a match, no questions asked. Sahil wouldn't have survived without them."

Arjun stared at her, his mind racing. "You mean... Sahil's liver..."

Mrs. Rao smiled grimly. "He got a new one three weeks ago. He's stable now. And alive."

The words hung in the air between them, heavy with implication. Arjun's heart pounded against his ribcage. **Sahil had been saved.** Not by the system, but by a network operating outside it. Illegal, dangerous, immoral—and undeniably effective.

"Who do I contact?" Arjun asked, the question slipping out before he could stop himself.

Mrs. Rao gave him a knowing look, as if she had been waiting for this moment. "I'll send you a number. You don't call. You text. They'll reach out when they're ready."

Arjun nodded numbly, his thoughts a tangled mess of fear, hope, and moral conflict. He knew the path he was about to step onto was dark and treacherous, but he also knew one undeniable truth: Aarav needed a heart, and this might be his only chance.

The next morning, the text message arrived—a single line with a phone number and the word: **"Send."** Arjun stared at his phone, the decision weighing on him like a stone. Once he sent the message, there would be no going back.

He thought about Meera, her tired eyes and fragile hope. He thought about Aarav, his small body struggling for every breath. The rules no longer seemed to matter. **What good were rules if they killed his child?**

With trembling fingers, Arjun typed the message:

"I need help."

He hit send.

For the next two days, Arjun carried his phone everywhere, waiting for a response. His nerves were frayed, every moment spent in agonizing anticipation. On the third day, the reply finally came.

"Midnight. Discretion required. Location to follow."

No signature. No further instructions. Just the promise of something dangerous lurking at the edge of the night.

Arjun stared at the screen, his heart hammering in his chest. **This was it. The first step into a world from which there was no escape.**

At midnight, Arjun stood in the shadows of a dimly lit alley, waiting. The street was quiet, the only sound the distant hum of traffic. His nerves were on edge, every muscle in his body coiled tight with tension.

A black sedan pulled up silently. The driver's window rolled down, and a man with sharp eyes and a cold smile motioned for Arjun to get in.

"You must be Dr. Malhotra," the man said smoothly. "Welcome. Let's talk about saving your son."

As Arjun climbed into the car, he knew he was crossing a line that could never be uncrossed. But the seed had already been planted, and it was now taking root, spreading through his soul like a dark vine.

There was no turning back.

Chapter 3: Meeting the Broker

Arjun sat in the backseat of the sleek black sedan, his heart pounding as the city lights blurred past the tinted windows. The man driving said nothing—only flicked glances at him through the rearview mirror, as if evaluating the passenger he had just picked up. The silence inside the car was suffocating, amplifying the sound of Arjun's heartbeat in his ears. With every passing second, the reality of what he was about to do sank deeper into his bones.

This wasn't just a meeting. This was a descent into a world most people never dared to imagine—a world where human organs were priced, packaged, and sold like contraband.

The car wound through darkened streets, eventually leaving the bustling core of the city. They entered a quieter district on the outskirts—warehouses, old factories, and shipping docks, long abandoned to the night. Arjun felt his stomach tighten with anxiety.

Finally, the sedan slowed to a stop in front of a nondescript building with no signs or lights, blending seamlessly with the other derelict structures.

THE ORGAN BROKER   17

The driver turned to face Arjun, his expression flat. "This is where you meet the Broker. Don't ask questions. Don't lie. And don't try to bargain."

Arjun swallowed hard and nodded.

The driver motioned toward a steel door. "He's waiting inside."

Arjun stepped out of the car, pulling his coat tighter against the night's chill. The door loomed ahead like a portal into another world. He hesitated for a moment, fighting the urge to turn back. But the image of Aarav—his pale, fragile body connected to tubes and monitors—flashed through his mind. That image pushed him forward.

He reached the door and gave it a light push. It swung open easily, revealing a dimly lit hallway that smelled of metal and antiseptic. With a deep breath, Arjun stepped inside, and the door clicked shut behind him with an ominous finality.

The hallway led to a small, windowless room where a single overhead light buzzed faintly. A man sat at a metal table in the center of the room, his posture relaxed but deliberate. He was tall, lean, and immaculately dressed in a tailored black suit that contrasted sharply with the drab surroundings. His dark eyes were sharp and calculating, as if they could strip a man down to his soul within seconds.

"Dr. Malhotra," the man said smoothly, gesturing for Arjun to sit. "I've heard a lot about you."

Arjun hesitated only for a moment before lowering himself into the cold metal chair. The man's presence radiated an unsettling calm—like a predator who knew he was in complete control.

"You can call me the Broker," the man said, his thin smile never reaching his eyes. "And I understand you have a problem. A problem I can solve."

Arjun clenched his hands under the table to stop them from trembling. "I need a heart. For my son."

The Broker gave a slow nod, as if they were discussing something as mundane as a business deal. "Yes. A heart. It can be arranged."

Arjun's throat tightened. "How? Where will it come from?"

The Broker raised an eyebrow, amused by the question. "Does it matter? A heart will be available—soon. But nothing in life is free, Dr. Malhotra. I assume you understand that."

A chill ran down Arjun's spine. "How much?"

The Broker leaned back in his chair, fingers steepled together. "Money is... part of the arrangement, yes. But we also deal in services. And you, Dr. Malhotra, possess a very valuable skill set."

Arjun's chest tightened with dread. "What kind of services?"

"Surgeries," the Broker said simply. "Discreet procedures, performed on clients who prefer to avoid the... complexities of the official healthcare system."

Arjun's stomach churned. He knew exactly what that meant—illegal operations, unregistered transplants, and who knew what else. Once he agreed, he would be complicit in a network that trafficked human lives.

The Broker's gaze sharpened, as if reading Arjun's thoughts. "I'm not offering this lightly. Our clients pay a premium for

THE ORGAN BROKER 19

anonymity and skill. In return, your son gets a heart. Quickly. Cleanly."

Arjun gripped the edge of the table, his knuckles white. "And if I say no?"

The Broker's smile vanished, replaced by an expression of cold indifference. "Then your son dies waiting for a miracle. And you live with the knowledge that you could have saved him, but chose not to."

The words hit Arjun like a punch to the gut. He sat in stunned silence, the weight of the choice pressing down on him like a lead blanket. He thought of Meera, of how hopeful she still was—still clinging to the belief that things would somehow work out.

But hope wouldn't save Aarav. Only a heart could.

"Where do the organs come from?" Arjun asked, his voice hollow.

The Broker's expression remained unreadable. "From those willing to give. Or those who no longer have a use for them. Does it really matter, Dr. Malhotra?"

Arjun felt nausea rise in his throat. He knew the truth—knew that most of the so-called donors were likely coerced, tricked, or simply discarded as collateral damage. But he was running out of time, and the world of ethics had no place in the fight to save his son.

"How many surgeries?" Arjun whispered, his voice barely audible.

The Broker leaned forward, his gaze unwavering. "Two. One transplant and one... extraction. Perform those for us, and the heart for your son will be delivered within days."

Arjun's mind reeled. **Extraction.** The word was clinical, but the meaning was clear. He would have to take an organ from someone—someone who might not survive the procedure.

He looked down at his hands, the same hands that had saved so many lives. Could he use them to take one away?

The Broker watched him in silence, his expression patient, as if he knew the decision had already been made.

Arjun closed his eyes, a wave of anguish crashing over him. There were no good choices—only bad ones and worse ones.

He thought of Aarav, gasping for breath in his hospital bed. Thought of the years he had dreamed of watching his son grow up, go to college, fall in love, and build a life of his own.

Those dreams were slipping away, and this deal—this horrifying, impossible deal—was the only way to pull them back from the edge.

When Arjun opened his eyes, they were filled with grim determination.

"I'll do it," he said, the words tasting like poison.

The Broker's smile returned, smooth and predatory. "Excellent. I knew you were a reasonable man."

He stood, extending a hand toward Arjun. "Welcome to our network, Dr. Malhotra. Your first assignment will arrive shortly."

Arjun hesitated for only a moment before taking the Broker's hand. It was cold, firm, and devoid of warmth.

In that moment, Arjun knew he had crossed a line he could never return from. The first cut had been made—and the only thing left was to see how deep the wound would go.

Chapter 4: Price Tag on Humanity

Arjun stood in the dimly lit, makeshift operating room, his gloved hands trembling as the overhead light cast a sterile glow on the lifeless body before him. The patient lay unconscious, prepped and ready for the transplant. Across the room, an anonymous surgical assistant—a wiry man with hollow eyes and a cold demeanor—adjusted the heart monitor, the beeping slow and mechanical, devoid of the emotional gravity that crushed Arjun's chest.

It had all felt surreal until this moment, as if he'd been drifting through a fever dream since he made his deal with the Broker. But now, with the scalpel resting heavily in his hand and the clock ticking down, the gravity of his decision struck him with suffocating force.

This wasn't the sterile, regulated world he knew. There were no nurses, no surgical protocols, and certainly no ethics board overseeing the procedure. The only thing that mattered here was results—an organ transferred from one body to another, a life saved in exchange for... what? The ruination of someone else's future? A price he wasn't prepared to understand?

He forced himself to focus. His mind needed to operate like it always had—with precision, clarity, and detachment.

But detachment was impossible when every fiber of his being screamed that this was wrong. **The human cost.** That thought hovered in his mind, refusing to be silenced.

The patient receiving the transplant was a young woman, no older than twenty-five. According to the Broker's associate, she was the daughter of a wealthy client, a girl born with a congenital heart defect. A legitimate heart from the official donor system wouldn't arrive in time to save her. So her family had turned to the black market—and to Arjun.

Arjun's instructions were simple: perform the transplant. Save the girl. Keep silent.

But the simplicity of the task was deceptive. The reality was far darker, messier, and filled with ethical landmines.

A second door in the corner of the room opened, and two men entered, dragging in a limp figure on a gurney. The person was unconscious, their thin body covered by a stained sheet. Arjun looked away, his breath catching in his throat.

The donor.

"Here's your heart," one of the men said gruffly, flipping the sheet back to reveal a gaunt young man—barely more than a boy. His skin was pale, his cheeks sunken, and a faint scar ran down his forearm.

Arjun's stomach twisted violently as he forced himself to look at the boy's face. The donor's chest rose and fell in shallow breaths, indicating that he was still alive—though barely.

"He's brain-dead," the assistant said flatly, as if that simple statement justified everything. "No family. No next of kin. He won't feel a thing."

The words were meant to reassure, but they had the opposite effect. Arjun knew better than most that the line between life and death wasn't as simple as flipping a switch. There was always something left—something unseen. **Every organ had a story.** And this boy's story was one that would never be told.

He felt bile rise in his throat as he thought about Aarav—his son, gasping for every breath, waiting for a heart that might never come. If Arjun hesitated now, if he walked away, this girl would die. But so, too, would Aarav. The cold calculus of the situation left no room for hesitation. One life for another. A trade. **A transaction with the highest possible stakes.**

"Doctor," the assistant said impatiently, glancing at the clock. "We need to move. His vitals won't hold much longer."

Arjun nodded, his mind reeling. The time for second-guessing was over. He was in too deep, and there was only one way forward—through the darkness.

The first incision was always the hardest. Arjun's hand trembled as he lowered the scalpel to the donor's chest, drawing a clean line down the sternum. The assistant worked quickly, prying open the rib cage with surgical clamps until the heart lay exposed—a fragile, beating organ, still clinging to life.

Arjun's gaze locked onto the heart. It was beautiful in a terrible, tragic way—a perfect engine, one that could have given the young man decades of life. Instead, it would be taken today, exchanged like currency to save someone else.

The assistant leaned in close. "No time for sentiment, Doctor. Extract it."

Arjun's hands moved mechanically, every motion guided by years of training. He cut through the arteries and veins, severing the heart from its host. The organ came free in his hands, warm and heavy, and for a moment, the world seemed to stand still. **This was the cost of survival. A life, reduced to a single organ.**

Without a word, Arjun handed the heart to the assistant, who placed it carefully into a preservation container. Time was of the essence. The recipient's chest had already been opened, and her frail, failing heart was removed and discarded in a steel tray.

Arjun stared at the lifeless heart in the tray, a lump forming in his throat. He had performed hundreds of transplants, but never like this. **This was theft.** A robbery of life itself.

He shook his head, forcing the thought away. There was no room for doubt now. The new heart was lowered into the young woman's chest, and Arjun set to work, stitching and reconnecting the arteries with practiced precision. His mind shut out everything but the task at hand—the rhythm of the sutures, the delicate balance of each connection.

For the next several hours, the room was silent except for the hum of machines and the occasional instructions from the assistant. Finally, the moment came—the heart was in place, and the time had come to see if it would beat.

"Prepare to defibrillate," Arjun whispered, his voice hoarse from hours of concentration.

The assistant placed the paddles on the girl's chest. Arjun pressed the button, sending a jolt of electricity through the heart. For a terrifying moment, nothing happened. Then, slowly, the heart shuddered and began to beat—weak at first, but steady.

THE ORGAN BROKER   25

A wave of relief washed over Arjun, but it was fleeting. The girl's life had been saved, but the price of that life was etched into the cold, lifeless body on the other gurney.

The assistant gave a satisfied nod. "Another successful operation, Doctor. The client will be pleased."

Arjun stared at the beating heart, feeling no sense of triumph—only a hollow emptiness. This wasn't a victory. It was a transaction, plain and simple.

After the surgery, Arjun stripped off his gloves and scrubbed his hands with a ferocity that bordered on violence. **No matter how much he washed, the blood would never truly come off.**

He avoided looking at the donor's body as the men prepared to wheel it away. He didn't want to know the boy's name, his story, or how he had ended up here. Knowing wouldn't change anything. It would only make the weight on Arjun's soul heavier.

The assistant approached him, wiping his hands on a stained towel. "You did well, Doctor. The first one is always the hardest. It gets easier."

Arjun shot him a glare, his stomach churning. "I don't want it to get easier."

The assistant smirked. "That's what they all say. At first."

Arjun said nothing, the words lodged painfully in his throat.

Later that night, as he sat alone in his car, the enormity of what he had done crashed down on him like a tidal wave. His hands shook uncontrollably, and for the first time in years, he felt the sting of tears in his eyes.

He had crossed a line—a line he could never uncross. The heart he had stolen tonight was not just a muscle. It was the embodiment of someone's future, someone's potential, someone's dreams. And he had taken it, all for the sake of saving another life.

He thought of Aarav, lying in his hospital bed, his tiny chest struggling with each breath. Arjun had made this choice for him, for his son. But at what cost?

His phone buzzed, pulling him from his spiraling thoughts. It was a message from the Broker.

"Well done, Dr. Malhotra. The first cut is the deepest. The heart for your son will be ready soon."

Arjun stared at the message, his hands trembling. The words felt like a noose tightening around his neck. There was no going back now.

He had made his choice.

And the price of that choice would haunt him forever.

Chapter 5: Ghosts on the Operating Table

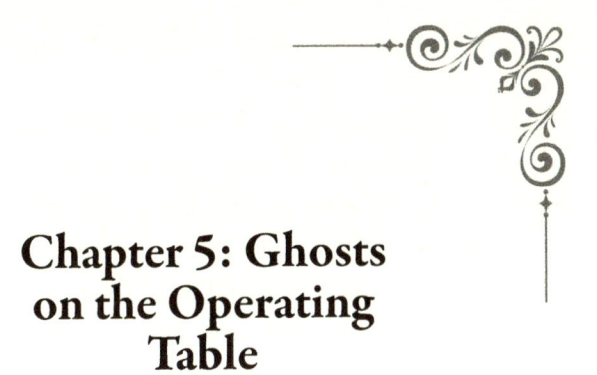

Arjun Malhotra stared at the ceiling of his bedroom, his eyes wide open despite the deep exhaustion clawing at his body. His wife, Meera, lay beside him, breathing softly in her sleep, unaware of the storm raging inside him. No matter how much he willed himself to drift off, sleep refused to come. Each time he closed his eyes, it was not darkness that welcomed him—it was the faces.

They haunted him—those faces. The boy whose heart he had removed in the underground operating room flashed behind his eyelids every time he blinked. His gaunt features, pale skin, and lifeless eyes were burned into Arjun's mind, a permanent stain he couldn't wash away. **He was gone now, but his heart beat inside someone else.** A stranger had survived, while the boy had been discarded like a piece of waste. And it was Arjun's hands that had made it happen.

He sat up with a jolt, running his trembling fingers through his hair. The bedside clock read 3:12 a.m. It had been three nights since the surgery, and Arjun hadn't slept for more than a handful of minutes at a time. Every time he drifted off, the ghosts of the operating table pulled him back, dragging him into a pit of guilt and shame.

A soft whimper broke the silence of the night, and Arjun turned toward Aarav's room down the hall. He slipped out of bed and padded silently toward his son's door, cracking it open just enough to peek inside.

Aarav lay tangled in his blankets, his small body shifting uncomfortably as he tried to find a restful position. His breathing was shallow and labored, even with the oxygen tube connected to his nose. The heart monitor beside his bed beeped steadily, each sound reminding Arjun how little time they had left.

He crossed the room and sat beside his son, brushing a strand of hair from the boy's clammy forehead. Aarav stirred slightly but didn't wake. Arjun closed his eyes, savoring the sound of his son's heartbeat—weak, but still there. **Still alive.** But how long could that fragile beat last without the heart that was promised?

Over the next few days, the ghosts followed Arjun everywhere. At the hospital, he went through the motions of his duties—consultations, surgeries, rounds—but his mind was elsewhere, caught in an endless loop of guilt. Every time he looked at a patient, he wondered: **How much is your life worth?**

The deal with the Broker had poisoned his thoughts, and now every interaction felt tainted. He saw potential donors in every waiting room, walking down every hallway—people who might one day find themselves on the wrong side of an underground transaction. **What separated them from the boy on the gurney? Luck? Money? Connections?**

He thought about the assistant's words the night of the surgery: **"He's brain-dead. No family."** At the time, Arjun had latched onto those words like a lifeline, clinging to the idea that the boy's life was already over. But now, in the quiet moments between tasks, the doubts gnawed at him.

What if it wasn't true?

What if the boy had a family, waiting somewhere, hoping he would come home? What if he wasn't brain-dead but merely sedated, his fate decided by people who saw him as nothing more than a commodity?

The questions swirled in Arjun's mind, each one darker than the last. He knew he couldn't ask the Broker. In this world, questions were dangerous, and curiosity was a liability. But the need for answers consumed him. He couldn't shake the feeling that there was more to these transactions than he had been told—that the victims weren't just faceless, nameless strangers, but real people with lives, dreams, and futures stolen from them.

One night, unable to bear the weight of his thoughts any longer, Arjun decided to investigate. He sat at his desk, his laptop glowing softly in the dark room, and began searching through medical databases. **Unregistered patients. Missing persons. Medical reports that didn't add up.** He scoured every corner of the internet,

Searched 4 sites

Arjun's sleepless nights bring him face-to-face with a sinister reality about the organ trade. His haunting doubts are not unfounded—many victims of illegal organ trafficking come from the world's most vulnerable populations, such as migrants, refugees, and individuals in extreme poverty. Reports show that some victims are lured under false pretenses, believing they will receive a job opportunity, only to wake up with an organ missing. Others are coerced, drugged, or sold by those who control them

Human Trafficking Search[1]

Alliance to End Human Trafficking[2]

.

This grim world is not merely the result of desperation on the recipient's end but a carefully orchestrated system involving organized criminal networks. The trade thrives because of the acute gap between organ supply and demand—only a fraction of those needing transplants receive them, making this illegal avenue increasingly lucrative. Medical professionals, from surgeons to ambulance drivers, have been implicated in these underground operations, hiding their activities within seemingly legitimate settings

UNODC[3]

.

The implications are staggering: once donors—whether willing or coerced—lose their organs, they often have no access to post-operative care. Their health deteriorates, and many are left unable to earn a livelihood, creating a ripple effect of poverty and hardship. Meanwhile, recipients of these

---

1. https://humantraffickingsearch.org/resource/trafficking-in-persons-for-the-purpose-of-organ-removal/

2. https://alliancetoendhumantrafficking.org/wp-content/uploads/2024/01/ATEHT-Human-Trafficking-Organ-Trafficking-EN-2024.pdf

3. https://www.unodc.org/unodc/frontpage/2024/June/explainer_-understanding-human-trafficking-for-organ-removal.html

black-market organs, often unaware of the crime behind their transplant, are rarely held accountable, perpetuating the cycle

Alliance to End Human Trafficking[4]
.

Arjun's mind spins with the weight of this knowledge. Every patient's survival now seems overshadowed by someone else's tragedy. Are these donors truly voluntary participants, or is the story much darker? The fine line between choice and coercion in the world of trafficking is one that Arjun struggles to comprehend. With each sleepless night, the ghosts on the operating table become more vivid, forcing him to confront whether he can continue down this path—and at what cost to his soul.

These revelations intensify the moral dilemmas gnawing at Arjun's conscience, as he realizes the transactional nature of human life in this world. This growing awareness adds another layer of tension to his journey, pushing him toward a dangerous precipice where every decision has profound consequences

Human Trafficking Search[5]

Alliance to End Human Trafficking[6]

As Arjun's sleepless nights drag on, the relentless presence of those ghostly faces—victims of organ trafficking—start to weigh heavily on his conscience. His late-night research, cross-referencing missing person reports and illicit transplant

---

4. https://alliancetoendhumantrafficking.org/wp-content/uploads/2024/01/ATEHT-Human-Trafficking-Organ-Trafficking-EN-2024.pdf

5. https://humantraffickingsearch.org/resource/trafficking-in-persons-for-the-purpose-of-organ-removal/

6. https://alliancetoendhumantrafficking.org/wp-content/uploads/2024/01/ATEHT-Human-Trafficking-Organ-Trafficking-EN-2024.pdf

operations, reveals disturbing truths. **The young men and women who disappear from shelters and migrant camps are often funneled into organ trafficking rings.** Vulnerable populations, including refugees, children, and the homeless, are particularly targeted

Human Trafficking Search[7]
Alliance to End Human Trafficking[8]
.

Each report Arjun reads tightens the knot in his chest. The horrifying consistency across stories gnaws at his mind: many victims are told they are "donating" in exchange for money that will never come. Some, unaware of what is happening to them, are sedated or kidnapped—waking up days later with a missing kidney or liver, weak and abandoned in some unfamiliar city

UNODC[9]
.

The boy whose heart Arjun transplanted weeks ago might have been one of these people. **Brain-dead? No family?** The phrases the Broker and his assistant had used to justify the theft echo in Arjun's mind. But what if the boy was merely homeless, undocumented, or had simply disappeared without anyone to notice his absence?

Moral Collapse

---

7. https://humantraffickingsearch.org/resource/trafficking-in-persons-for-the-purpose-of-organ-removal/

8. https://alliancetoendhumantrafficking.org/wp-content/uploads/2024/01/ATEHT-Human-Trafficking-Organ-Trafficking-EN-2024.pdf

9. https://www.unodc.org/unodc/frontpage/2024/June/explainer_-understanding-human-trafficking-for-organ-removal.html

THE ORGAN BROKER

Every day, Arjun goes through the motions at the hospital, but his work no longer feels the same. The patients he treats seem like shadows, their lives entangled with unknown fates. **For every heart that beats, another has stopped.** This new truth sinks into his soul, deeper than the scalpel's edge ever could. And as he wrestles with the implications, he begins questioning his every decision.

At home, Aarav's condition deteriorates further. Watching his son struggle for every breath twists the knife in Arjun's conscience. **How can he wrestle with these moral questions when his own child is dying?** In the end, isn't saving Aarav worth any price? **Or does that very thought make him no better than the traffickers he now abhors?**

But the boy's face—thin, pallid, and innocent—refuses to leave Arjun's mind. His name might never be known, his story forever untold, but his presence lingers, a reminder of what Arjun has sacrificed to secure Aarav's future.

Confronting the Broker

One sleepless night, driven by guilt and needing to understand the truth, Arjun sends a message to the Broker: **"Where did the heart come from? Was the donor truly brain-dead?"**

The reply comes quickly, as if the Broker had been expecting this:

"Does it matter? The heart saved your son. Focus on what you've gained, not what you've lost."

Arjun stares at the message, his hands trembling. **He realizes, with chilling clarity, that the Broker's world is built on a deliberate erasure of humanity.** There are no names, no histories—only organs and transactions. The people who die in this system aren't just bodies—they are stories that are silenced, lives that are erased for the sake of others' survival.

A New Nightmare

The ghosts begin appearing during surgeries. As Arjun performs even routine procedures, he sees flashes of faces—young men, women, even children—lying on the operating table, their vacant eyes fixed on him. Their presence isn't angry or vengeful; it is worse—they are resigned, as if they knew their fates had been sealed the moment they were chosen.

During a cardiac bypass on a patient, Arjun falters for the first time in his career. His hands freeze, his mind locking up as he imagines the boy's heart beating beneath the girl's ribcage—**a heart ripped from a life just as worthy, just as precious as Aarav's.**

The attending nurse notices Arjun's hesitation. "Doctor? Are you okay?"

He nods quickly, shaking off the vision, forcing himself to complete the procedure. But the encounter leaves him shaken. **He can no longer trust his own hands—not when they have taken as much as they have given.**

Meera's Fears

Meera notices the changes in Arjun. The distance in his eyes, the long nights he spends staring into nothingness, the way he avoids looking at Aarav's chest whenever their son lifts his shirt to show his scar from a recent procedure.

"Arjun," she says gently one night, placing a hand on his shoulder, "what's happening to you? You saved him... shouldn't you be relieved?"

Arjun swallows hard, his throat tight with guilt. **How can he tell Meera that the heart beating inside Aarav might have** come from a boy who never chose to give it up?** How can he confess that every heartbeat their son takes feels like a betrayal of someone else's future?

"I'm just tired," Arjun whispers. It's not a lie, but it's far from the truth.

The Breaking Point

The next time the Broker contacts Arjun, it's not to congratulate him but to offer another job. Another surgery, another organ to transplant. **"The client is paying well,"** the Broker tells him. **"You've proven yourself. Now it's time to build on that trust."**

Arjun wants to refuse, to walk away from the darkness that is slowly consuming him. But the Broker's words are as sharp as a scalpel: **"You still owe us, Doctor. Or did you think debts like these disappear once the first heart beats?"**

The truth is undeniable: Arjun is trapped. **He thought the first cut would be the hardest—but every cut after that only deepens the wound.** There's no way out, not without consequences that would shatter everything he holds dear.

Chapter 6: Into the Underworld

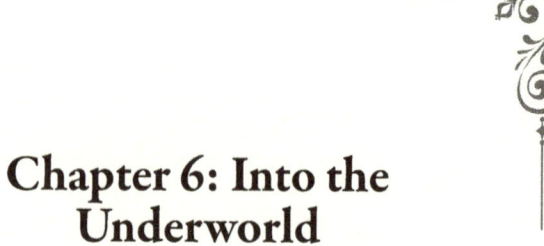

The airport was bustling with travelers—families, tourists, and businesspeople all moving with purpose. But as Arjun Malhotra wheeled his suitcase through the terminal, it felt like he was walking deeper into a labyrinth where every exit led further away from the light. His destination wasn't marked on any tourist map, and the people he was about to meet didn't appear in government databases. **He was leaving behind the last remnants of his former life and stepping into the unknown—a place where morality was currency and human lives were traded like stocks.**

His phone buzzed with a message from the Broker: **"A car will pick you up in Istanbul. Your contact will introduce you to our international partners."**

Istanbul. A city that straddled two continents, where East met West, and where shadows stretched long beneath the ancient domes and modern skyscrapers. It was an ideal meeting ground for those in the black-market organ trade—a place where borders blurred, both geographically and morally.

Arjun boarded his flight in silence, his heart heavy with the knowledge of what lay ahead. He thought of Aarav, of the heart beating inside his son's chest—a heart stolen from a nameless boy. **If that was the cost to save his child, what new price would he have to pay to secure his freedom?**

A World Beneath the Surface

When the plane touched down in Istanbul, Arjun was greeted by a man in a dark suit holding a sign with his name. The driver's expression was unreadable, and his silence only added to the weight pressing on Arjun's chest. They drove through the bustling city streets until they reached a sleek, modern hotel on the Bosphorus. But this was only a resting place; the real journey would begin at night.

As promised, a different car arrived at midnight. This time, the driver took Arjun away from the glittering lights of the city and into its underbelly—a maze of narrow streets and forgotten neighborhoods. **The glamour of Istanbul vanished, replaced by graffiti-covered walls and silent alleyways where deals were made in hushed whispers.**

Eventually, the car stopped in front of an unmarked building. The driver nodded toward the door. "This is where it begins."

Arjun stepped out, his nerves fraying with every step toward the entrance. **What was he walking into?**

The Humanitarian Façade

Inside, the room looked more like an office of a charitable foundation than the headquarters of an organ-trafficking network. Banners on the walls displayed slogans about healthcare access and medical aid, written in multiple languages. Pamphlets promised assistance for refugees and victims of natural disasters. The smiling faces on the posters hinted at hope, but Arjun knew better—**this was hope with a hidden cost.**

A tall woman greeted him, her smile warm but her eyes cold. "Dr. Malhotra. Welcome. I'm Selin." She extended a hand, her grip firm and practiced.

Arjun tried to keep his voice steady. "You run a... foundation?"

Selin's smile didn't falter. "We provide solutions, Doctor. Healthcare where it's needed most. We deal in logistics that governments can't handle."

Arjun understood the subtext immediately. **"Logistics" was just a euphemism for organ trafficking.** The foundation was a cover—a way to disguise their operations under the veneer of humanitarian aid. Refugee camps, disaster zones, and impoverished communities were their hunting grounds, where people were desperate enough to sell anything, including their bodies.

Selin led Arjun through the office, passing by desks where employees tapped on computers or made phone calls. Everything looked ordinary—just another NGO doing good work. But the conversations Arjun overheard hinted at something far darker.

"Two kidneys already secured in Lebanon, waiting for transport..."

"Surgeon on standby in Bangkok, transplant scheduled for tomorrow..."

"The liver donor... yes, they signed consent papers. No, they didn't read them."

Arjun's stomach churned as the truth settled in. **This wasn't just a trade—it was an industry.**

Meeting the Players

THE ORGAN BROKER

Selin escorted Arjun to a conference room where several men and women were already seated. They introduced themselves casually—doctors, brokers, and logistics managers, each playing a role in the operation. Some wore expensive suits, others dressed casually, as if they were attending a business seminar rather than orchestrating illegal transplants.

The introductions were brief. Arjun was there for one reason—to prove himself. **His surgical skills had bought his son's heart, but now they demanded more.** He was expected to perform surgeries for their network across multiple countries, ensuring transplants were completed without complications.

A man named Viktor, a Russian logistics manager, leaned back in his chair, observing Arjun with a predatory smile. "You'll find that this business has few rules, Doctor. But the most important one is simple: success. Our clients pay for outcomes, not excuses."

Arjun nodded, his jaw tight. He understood. **Failure was not an option.**

Into the Operating Rooms of the Shadows

Over the next few days, Arjun's nightmare deepened. He traveled to secret clinics in obscure locations—abandoned hospitals, private villas converted into surgical theaters, even yachts outfitted with operating rooms. Each setting was more surreal than the last, a patchwork of opulence and decay where human lives were treated as commodities.

The surgeries he performed varied—from kidney extractions on sedated donors to heart transplants for billionaires who refused to wait on official lists. Every procedure was carried out under strict secrecy. No patient names, no donor histories, just numbers on a chart and organs waiting to be moved.

The first time Arjun operated on a donor who was fully awake—too poor to afford anesthesia—he almost walked away. But the thought of Aarav kept him rooted to the spot. **If he didn't do the surgery, someone else would. And that person might not care whether the donor lived or died.**

The donors often came from the margins of society—**undocumented migrants, prisoners, or refugees fleeing war-torn regions.** Many were coerced into signing consent forms they didn't understand, while others had no idea what was being taken from them until it was too late

Alliance to End Human Trafficking[1]

.

One night, after performing a liver extraction on a young Syrian refugee, Arjun sat in the corner of the makeshift operating room, his hands covered in blood. **The boy had cried for his mother until the anesthesia knocked him out.** When the surgery was over, he was taken away, his fate unknown.

Arjun buried his face in his hands, feeling the weight of every life he had touched—and every life he had destroyed.

A Harder Path to Freedom

The deeper Arjun ventured into this world, the harder it became to imagine a way out. **The network was too vast, too powerful.** The people he worked with weren't just criminals—they were well-connected professionals, some with ties to governments and hospitals. Walking away from them wasn't just dangerous—it was impossible.

---

1. https://alliancetoendhumantrafficking.org/wp-content/uploads/2024/01/ATEHT-Human-Trafficking-Organ-Trafficking-EN-2024.pdf

Every time he thought about leaving, the Broker reminded him of the debt he owed. "Your son's heart bought you entry into this world," the Broker told him during a phone call. "But if you want to leave, you'll need to pay in more than just skills."

Arjun knew what that meant. **Leaving would cost him his freedom—or his life.**

Chapter 7: Blood Money

Arjun sat in the dimly lit hotel room, staring at his trembling hands. They were steady in the operating room, but outside, in the silence of the night, they betrayed him. **He couldn't stop thinking about where the organs were coming from.** Not just abstractly, but in vivid detail—faces, bodies, lives uprooted and stolen to make transplants possible. Each heart, kidney, and liver he extracted weighed on his soul like a brick. **What price had others paid for his child to live?**

Over the last few weeks, he had been operating in the shadows—moving from one clinic to another, ferrying between Istanbul, Bangkok, and Nairobi. With each surgery, Arjun saw the disturbing truth with increasing clarity: **the organ trade was built on the suffering of the most vulnerable.**

The deeper he ventured into the network, the more stories he uncovered—stories too harrowing to forget. **These weren't just anonymous bodies—these were people who had been promised freedom, survival, or security, only to end up on the operating table.** And Arjun, though reluctant, was now complicit in their exploitation.

The Refugees

It started in refugee camps. Arjun saw it firsthand when he was taken to an illegal clinic on the outskirts of Athens. The clinic operated just beyond the reach of the law, tucked into an abandoned building near a refugee settlement.

A young Syrian man lay on the table, his dark eyes filled with terror. His gaunt body told the story of years spent in war zones and refugee camps, running from one nightmare to another. Arjun overheard snippets of conversation as the clinic staff prepped the operating room.

"He thought we'd smuggle him to Europe if he gave us a kidney," one nurse said with a shrug. "Poor fool didn't know the kidney was the ticket, not the destination."

Arjun felt his throat tighten. **The man had sold his kidney for the promise of freedom.** Instead, he was being discarded like a used tool. There would be no ticket, no new life—only a scar and a lifetime of regret. **For every organ sold, there was a promise broken.**

The surgery went smoothly, and the kidney was packed in ice, ready for transport to a wealthy recipient in London. As the anesthetic wore off, the young man awoke, groggy and disoriented. His lips moved, but no sound came out. **Arjun knew the words he was trying to say: "Where am I? What happens next?"** But there were no answers. The man was already forgotten.

The Prisoners

In Bangkok, Arjun was taken to another clinic—a high-security operation that catered to international clients.

The donors this time were prisoners, men serving life sentences in overcrowded jails.

"They volunteered," one of the surgeons told Arjun with a grim smile, though there was no humor in his eyes. "Reduced sentence in exchange for an organ. Sounds fair, right?"

But Arjun knew better. **The prisoners weren't volunteering—they were being coerced.** With no way out of their desperate circumstances, many chose to part with a kidney or part of their liver in the hope of reducing their sentence. **It was a devil's bargain, with no guarantee that the authorities would honor their end of the deal.**

During one procedure, Arjun looked down at the donor—a middle-aged man with tattoos marking his years behind bars. **The man didn't beg or cry—he simply stared at the ceiling, resigned to his fate.**

Arjun's hands moved methodically as he extracted the organ, but his mind was in turmoil. **What justice could exist in a world where prisoners were harvested for spare parts?** How far had he fallen that he now participated in such atrocities?

The Children

The worst realization came in Nairobi, where Arjun was introduced to another segment of the trade—**the trafficking of children for organs.**

He had been summoned to a private estate on the outskirts of the city, where a client awaited a liver transplant for their child. The donor, as always, was already prepped and sedated by the time Arjun arrived.

But when he saw the donor on the table, his breath caught in his throat. **The donor was no older than ten—a child.**

He turned to the assistant in disbelief. "Where did they get this child?"

The assistant's reply was cold and matter-of-fact. "He's an orphan. Picked up off the streets. No one will miss him."

Arjun felt the room spin. **A child—just like Aarav.** But unlike his son, this boy had no one to fight for him. No one to care whether he lived or died. **This boy's life would end here, in silence, so that another child could live.**

For a moment, Arjun froze, unable to move. He thought of Aarav, safe in his hospital bed, his chest rising and falling with the stolen gift of life. **How could he save one child by sacrificing another?**

The assistant noticed Arjun's hesitation. "Doctor, we don't have time for this. You knew what you signed up for."

Arjun forced himself to breathe, forced himself to steady his hands. **This was the cost of saving lives.** And yet, every cut he made felt like a betrayal of everything he once believed in.

The Breaking Point

Days turned into weeks, and with each surgery, the weight on Arjun's conscience grew heavier. **He had entered this world to save Aarav, but now he was drowning in blood—blood that no amount of scrubbing could wash away.**

One night, after finishing yet another operation on a trafficked donor, Arjun sat alone in his hotel room, his hands shaking uncontrollably. **He couldn't do this anymore.** Every face, every scar, every stolen life haunted him. The refugees, the prisoners, the children—they had become ghosts, following him everywhere he went.

He picked up his phone, fingers trembling, and called the Broker.

"I'm done," Arjun whispered. "I can't do this anymore."

The Broker's voice on the other end was calm, almost amused. "There is no 'done,' Dr. Malhotra. You knew that the moment you made the first cut."

Arjun closed his eyes, feeling the walls close in around him. **He was trapped.** The only way out was through—deeper into the darkness, until there was nothing left of the man he used to be.

Chapter 8: The Anatomy of Betrayal

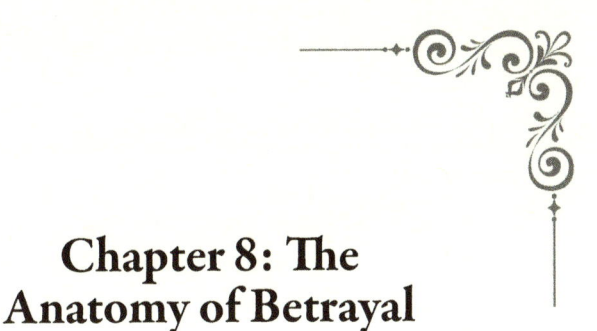

Arjun Malhotra sat in his office, lost in thought as the hospital buzzed around him. The familiar hum of medical equipment and the murmur of nurses felt distant, like a dream barely within reach. It was a facade—everything in his life had become a facade. He had ventured too deep into the underworld of illegal organ trafficking, a place where the lines between right and wrong had dissolved. **His life was now an intricate web of deceit, and the walls were beginning to close in.**

He sensed something was off before it happened—an intuition born of fear and guilt. **He had been too careful, or so he thought.** No one was supposed to know about his involvement with the Broker and the black market. Yet, in the past few days, strange things had begun to happen—subtle shifts that felt like warning signs. Colleagues grew quieter around him. Meetings ended abruptly when he walked into a room. **His phone calls were being dropped too often, and his emails went unanswered.**

But the final blow came when his closest ally—Dr. Kothari, a senior cardiologist and someone he had confided in more than once—stopped by his office with a grim expression.

"Arjun," Kothari began, closing the door behind him, "we need to talk."

Arjun's stomach tightened. **This was it.**

The Leak

Kothari lowered himself into the chair across from Arjun's desk, his brow furrowed with concern. "There's a rumor going around," he said slowly, choosing his words carefully. "Some of the nurses overheard something... something that could be very dangerous for you."

Arjun leaned forward, his pulse quickening. "What are you talking about?"

Kothari hesitated, then exhaled sharply. "There's talk that you've been... involved in things outside the hospital. Illegal things."

Arjun's heart stopped. He knew exactly what Kothari was referring to, but hearing it out loud made it feel all too real.

"Someone's been talking," Kothari continued. "It's been subtle, but the rumors are spreading fast. The administration has already started poking around. And if they find out what you've been up to..."

Arjun clenched his fists, trying to keep his composure. **Who could have leaked it?** He had been meticulous—careful with every message, every conversation. The Broker's network promised discretion. But promises were fragile things in this world.

"Do you know who's spreading this?" Arjun asked, his voice low and tight.

Kothari shook his head. "Not yet. But the staff is buzzing. And if someone in administration gets wind of it..." He didn't finish the sentence, but Arjun knew what he meant. **It wouldn't just be his job on the line—he could go to prison.**

Kothari leaned closer, his eyes filled with concern. "Listen to me, Arjun. If there's any truth to these rumors—if you're involved in something you shouldn't be—you need to cut ties. Now."

Arjun forced a bitter smile. **There was no cutting ties.** The Broker didn't let people walk away, not without consequences. But he couldn't tell Kothari that.

"I'll handle it," Arjun said quietly. "Thanks for the warning."

Kothari gave him a long, searching look, then nodded. "Be careful, my friend. You're walking a dangerous path."

As Kothari left the office, Arjun's mind raced. **Someone knew. Someone was talking.** And if he didn't act fast, everything would unravel.

Paranoia and Pressure

The paranoia began to consume Arjun. Every glance from a colleague felt like an accusation. Every phone call made him jump. **He couldn't trust anyone.** Even Meera noticed the change in him, though she didn't know the cause.

"You're so distracted lately," she said one evening as they sat by Aarav's bedside. "What's going on, Arjun?"

He forced a smile, brushing her concerns aside. **How could he explain that their son's survival was tied to a world of crime and betrayal?** How could he tell her that their family's happiness came at the expense of someone else's life? He couldn't. So, he kept the truth buried, even as it gnawed at him from the inside.

A Visit from the Authorities

It happened two days later. Arjun was making his rounds when two men in plain clothes appeared at the hospital's entrance, flashing badges to the security guard.

The police.

They moved with purpose, their expressions grim as they scanned the hallways. **They were looking for someone.** And Arjun knew—**they were looking for him.**

He ducked into an empty patient room, his heart hammering in his chest. **This was happening too fast.** He thought he had more time to figure things out, but now the authorities were here, and the walls were closing in.

From his hiding place, he saw the men approach the nurse's station, speaking to one of the supervisors. The conversation was brief, but it was enough to send chills down Arjun's spine.

"They're asking questions about me," he whispered to himself. **How much did they know?**

The Anatomy of Betrayal

Arjun paced the room, his mind racing through possibilities. **Had the Broker betrayed him? Or was it someone at the hospital—someone who had pieced things together?** The network promised anonymity, but in a world driven by greed, betrayal was inevitable. **Whoever had leaked his involvement wasn't just endangering his career—they were putting his life on the line.**

Arjun knew he needed to act fast. **The Broker didn't tolerate exposure.** If the authorities got too close, the network would cut its losses—and that included cutting Arjun loose. Permanently.

THE ORGAN BROKER

His phone buzzed in his pocket, and he pulled it out with trembling hands. It was a message from the Broker:

"We have a problem. Handle it, or we will."

The message was clear. **The Broker knew about the leak—and the consequences were now Arjun's to bear.**

Allies or Enemies?

Arjun's paranoia deepened as he tried to figure out who had betrayed him. **Could it have been Kothari?** No—Kothari wouldn't have warned him if he was behind the leak. But someone else at the hospital knew.

He thought of the staff members he had worked with—the ones who might have seen or heard something they shouldn't have. **Had one of the nurses overheard a conversation? Or had someone noticed the late-night phone calls, the strange absences?**

Arjun's world was unraveling, and he didn't know who to trust. Even Meera, with her worried glances and probing questions, began to feel like a threat. **What if she found out? What if she couldn't forgive him for the choices he had made?**

The weight of betrayal pressed down on him from all sides. **He was trapped in a web of lies, and every thread was starting to unravel.**

Running Out of Time

Arjun knew he needed to act quickly. **The police were circling, and the Broker's patience was wearing thin.** He couldn't afford to make a mistake—not now, when everything was on the line.

He slipped out of the hospital through a back entrance, his heart pounding as he made his way to the parking lot. **He needed to disappear, at least for a little while.** If he stayed in one place for too long, the authorities would find him—and so would the network.

As he drove through the city, his mind raced with questions. **Who had betrayed him? And how could he escape the consequences?**

There were no easy answers—only hard choices and impossible odds. **And the worst part was knowing that, in the end, he might not be able to save himself.**

Chapter 9: A Knife to the Throat

Arjun's phone buzzed in the dead of night, its harsh vibration shattering the fragile quiet that hung over his home. He had been sitting by Aarav's bedside, watching his son sleep, cherishing each precious heartbeat that the stolen heart provided. But when he saw the name on the screen—**The Broker**—his stomach twisted in knots. The calls from the Broker were always bad news. **This time, it would be worse.**

With trembling fingers, Arjun answered.

"Dr. Malhotra," the smooth, clinical voice said. There was no preamble, no room for small talk. "We have a new situation. You're going to help us resolve it."

Arjun closed his eyes. **How many more surgeries? How many more lives would be stolen or broken in this twisted web?** "I told you I'm done," he whispered, gripping the phone so tightly it hurt. "I can't keep doing this."

"You're not done," the Broker replied coldly. "You owe us."

Arjun's throat tightened. **He knew there was no way out—not until the Broker decided to release him.**

"What do you want?" Arjun asked, already fearing the answer.

There was a brief silence on the other end of the line, the kind that felt calculated, designed to raise the tension.

"We need you to perform a surgery," the Broker finally said. "A rival's family member—his brother. It's a delicate procedure, and you're the only one we trust to handle it."

Arjun's heart raced. **A rival? This wasn't just about money anymore—this was something far more dangerous.**

"What happens if I say no?" Arjun asked, though he already knew the answer.

The Broker's voice dropped into a quiet, lethal tone. "If you refuse, your son's heart becomes a liability. And we don't tolerate liabilities."

Arjun's blood ran cold. **The heart—the one thing keeping Aarav alive—was a constant reminder of his debt to the network.** Refusing the Broker wasn't just dangerous; it was suicide.

A Choice Without Options

Arjun paced the room, his mind racing through the possibilities. **If he refused, Aarav's heart would become a ticking time bomb—one the Broker wouldn't hesitate to detonate.** But if he agreed, he would be stepping even deeper into a world of violence and corruption.

Performing surgery for a rival? That meant crossing a line he had never imagined—**entering into a personal feud where lives were currency and grudges were settled with scalpels instead of bullets.** And the worst part was knowing that this wasn't about saving lives—it was about leverage, power, and control.

His hands shook as he sat down on the couch, burying his face in his hands. **How much more could he give before he**

lost himself entirely? Every surgery had taken a piece of his soul, and now there was almost nothing left. But he couldn't walk away—not when Aarav's life was on the line.

The Meeting

The next day, a black SUV pulled up outside the hospital to take Arjun to the location where the surgery would take place. The driver didn't speak, and Arjun didn't ask any questions. **He knew better by now.**

They drove for hours, leaving the bustling city behind and heading toward the countryside. The landscape grew barren and desolate, a fitting reflection of the hopelessness that gnawed at Arjun's heart.

Finally, the car pulled up to a gated estate. The building was sleek and modern, with high walls and cameras watching every corner. **This wasn't just a home—it was a fortress.**

The guard at the gate let them in without a word, and Arjun was escorted inside by two men with cold, expressionless faces. **He was in the enemy's den now, and every step felt like walking into a trap.**

The Patient

Inside, Arjun was led to a private medical suite—an operating room disguised as part of the luxurious estate. The air smelled faintly of antiseptic, and the surgical tools were laid out on a pristine metal tray.

The patient was already on the table, sedated and prepped for surgery. **The man was young, no older than thirty, with tattoos marking his allegiance to a criminal faction—probably the rival group the Broker had mentioned.**

Arjun's throat tightened as he stared down at the unconscious man. **This wasn't just a surgery—it was a message.** The man's life hung in the balance, and whether he lived or died would determine the outcome of a dangerous feud.

The assistant standing beside Arjun handed him a pair of gloves. "You know the drill," the assistant said with a smirk. "No complications, no questions."

Arjun forced himself to nod. **He was a surgeon—he had to focus on the procedure, not the politics.** But it was easier said than done.

A Surgery Under Duress

As Arjun worked, the silence in the room was deafening. Every movement felt weighted, every breath a struggle against the tension that coiled around him like a noose.

The procedure was complex—a bullet wound that had damaged the man's liver and diaphragm. **Arjun's hands moved with practiced precision, but his mind was elsewhere—haunted by the knowledge that this surgery wasn't about healing.** It was about survival—his own, his son's, and now the man's on the table.

For hours, Arjun fought to keep the man alive, stitching, clamping, and repairing tissue with the same care he would give to any patient. But as he worked, a dark thought crept into his mind: **What if he let the man die?**

What if, by making one small mistake, he could end this nightmare? The man would die, and the feud between the Broker's network and its rival might end. Arjun could walk away, free of the debt that had consumed his life.

The scalpel hovered in his hand, trembling slightly. **One slip—just one—and it would all be over.**

But then he thought of Aarav, lying in his hospital bed, his heart beating steadily with the stolen gift of life. **Could he really gamble with his son's future? Could he risk everything for the sake of revenge?**

With a shuddering breath, Arjun refocused. **He couldn't do it.** No matter how deep he was in, no matter how broken he felt, he was still a doctor. **And doctors saved lives—even when those lives didn't deserve saving.**

The Aftermath

When the surgery was over, Arjun stepped back, his hands trembling from exhaustion and fear. **The man on the table was alive—for now.** The assistant gave him a nod, as if to say, "Good enough."

Arjun stripped off his gloves and washed his hands, but no amount of scrubbing could erase the feeling of dirt on his skin. **He had done what the Broker asked—but at what cost?**

As he left the operating room, one of the guards handed him a phone. It was a direct line to the Broker.

"It's done," Arjun said, his voice hollow.

"Good," the Broker replied. "You've proven yourself again, Doctor. Your son's heart will continue to beat—for now."

The line went dead, and Arjun stood there in the silent hallway, feeling more trapped than ever. **Every surgery, every life saved or lost, tightened the noose around his neck.** And he knew, with chilling certainty, that the next demand from the Broker would be even worse.

There was no end to this. No escape. **Only deeper darkness—and a knife forever at his throat.**

Chapter 10: Fractured Oaths

The hospital lights buzzed faintly above Arjun as he stared into the operating room window, the scene inside both familiar and alien. **This was supposed to be his sanctuary—a place where healing happened, where his hands worked miracles.** But now it felt like a battlefield, each procedure a painful reminder of the promises he had broken.

His thoughts returned to the night he first took the Hippocratic Oath—the vow to do no harm, to save lives without prejudice or personal interest. He had stood among his peers, reciting those sacred words with a sense of purpose. Back then, the idea of betraying that oath had seemed impossible. **Medicine was supposed to be his calling, his way of giving back, not a burden that would shatter his soul.**

Yet here he was—a man torn between two identities. **A father who would do anything to save his son, and a doctor who had become a shadow of the man he once was.** How had it come to this?

The Ghosts of Promises Broken

The stolen heart that now beat inside Aarav's chest had saved his son's life, but it came at an unthinkable cost. **Every** beat reminded Arjun that he had betrayed someone else's future. He tried to rationalize it, telling himself that the donor had been brain-dead, a boy with no future to speak of. But the truth lingered like a knife pressed against his heart: **He hadn't asked enough questions.** He hadn't wanted to know the story behind that heart because knowing would make the weight of his guilt unbearable.

It wasn't just the surgeries that haunted him—it was the faces of the donors he could no longer forget. Refugees, prisoners, children—**each of them had been someone with a life, a story, a future stolen to buy time for someone else.** Was his son's life more valuable than theirs? Did his love for Aarav justify the horrors he had committed?

His hands, once steady and certain, now felt foreign to him. They were tools he no longer trusted. **What good was a doctor who couldn't tell if he was saving a life or destroying one?**

Confronting the Mirror

One night, unable to bear the weight of his thoughts, Arjun found himself standing in front of the bathroom mirror. The man staring back at him was a stranger—**tired, gaunt, and haunted.** There were lines on his face that hadn't been there before, the shadow of stubble on his jaw, and an emptiness in his eyes that no amount of rest could fill.

He splashed cold water on his face, but it didn't help. The memories were still there—the young boy on the gurney, the Syrian refugee with tears in his eyes, the child trafficked for parts. **All of them had been sacrificed on the altar of survival, and Arjun had been the high priest wielding the scalpel.**

As he stared into his own reflection, a question clawed its way to the surface of his mind: **Who am I now?**

A Conversation with Meera

Meera found him sitting in the dark later that night, his head in his hands. **She had been watching him closely, sensing the change in him but never asking the questions that lingered on her lips.** But tonight, she couldn't stay silent any longer.

"Arjun," she whispered, sitting beside him. "What's happening to you? You've been... distant. Ever since Aarav's surgery, it's like you're not really here."

He looked at her, the love of his life, the mother of his child, and for a moment, the truth hovered on the tip of his tongue. **He wanted to tell her everything—that their son's life had been bought with blood, that every beat of Aarav's heart was a stolen gift.**

But the words wouldn't come. Instead, he said, "I did what I had to do."

Meera's brow furrowed. "What does that mean?"

"It means..." He paused, his voice heavy with guilt. "It means some things can't be undone. No matter how much you want them to."

Meera reached for his hand, her touch warm and grounding. "Whatever it is, Arjun, you don't have to carry it alone."

But he knew that wasn't true. **Some burdens were too dark to share.**

The Reckoning

THE ORGAN BROKER

The next day, as Arjun prepared for yet another surgery, the weight of his decisions pressed down on him harder than ever. **This patient was just another person on the receiving end of the system—a wealthy businessman who had jumped the waiting list thanks to Arjun's connections.**

As he scrubbed in, his hands trembled. **The thought of performing another surgery, of contributing further to the chain of exploitation, made him feel sick.** He had become everything he once swore he wouldn't—**a doctor who prioritized survival over ethics, power over compassion.**

The nurse beside him noticed his hesitation. "Are you all right, Doctor?"

Arjun nodded mechanically, but inside, he knew he wasn't. **He wasn't sure if he would ever be all right again.**

The Moment of Truth

The surgery began, and Arjun's hands moved with practiced precision, but his mind was elsewhere—**lost in the labyrinth of his guilt.** The ghost of the boy whose heart now beat inside Aarav lingered in the corners of his vision, silent but accusing. **Every suture felt like a betrayal. Every cut felt like a confession.**

At one point, his scalpel hovered over an artery, and for a fleeting moment, Arjun considered stopping—**just walking away from the table and never looking back.** But he knew it wouldn't be that easy. **The Hippocratic Oath demanded that he finish what he had started.** But the oath also demanded that he do no harm, and that was the part that haunted him most of all.

Was it worse to let someone die because of his refusal to act? Or to save them knowing that someone else had already paid the price for their life?

The Question of the Soul

By the time the surgery ended, Arjun felt like a shell of a man—**a ghost trapped in a body that no longer felt like his own.** As he stripped off his gloves and washed his hands, he thought about the price of survival. **It wasn't just blood that stained his hands—it was his soul.**

He had spent his life believing that being a doctor meant healing the sick and saving lives. But now, he wasn't so sure. **Was saving Aarav worth losing his soul?** If the answer was yes, what kind of man did that make him? And if the answer was no, what kind of father would he be?

These questions consumed him, gnawing at his conscience like a relentless tide. **The more he tried to find clarity, the more lost he became.** Every path led deeper into the darkness, and there were no maps to guide him out.

Chapter 11: Shattered Masks

Arjun had long suspected that the black-market organ trade was larger than it appeared—a network operating across borders, supplying illegal transplants for the wealthy and powerful. But the depth of corruption he uncovered shattered the last remnants of his belief in the medical system. **What he thought was an underground operation run by desperate criminals was, in reality, a well-oiled machine fueled by doctors, hospitals, government officials, and corporate interests.**

It all began with a document—a seemingly innocuous spreadsheet he found tucked inside the papers handed to him by one of the network's brokers. At first, the numbers and initials meant nothing. But as Arjun delved deeper, the pieces began to fall into place, revealing a vast conspiracy that spanned continents and thrived under the guise of legitimacy.

The First Thread Unravels

Arjun sat at his desk late one night, exhausted but driven by the need to understand the scope of the operation he had unwittingly become a part of. He scanned the spreadsheet again, following a trail of names and payments that crisscrossed through several countries. **The numbers didn't just represent surgeries—they were payouts, coded to cover expenses for bribery, transportation, and medical services.**

One name in particular stood out—**Dr. Janice Halloran**, a renowned transplant specialist and professor at a prestigious American university. Arjun knew her by reputation—**she had once been a mentor to some of his colleagues, hailed as a pioneer in ethical organ transplantation.** But her name appeared in the ledger repeatedly, listed under columns marked "facilitation" and "consultation."

It didn't make sense. **Why would a doctor of her stature be involved in something like this?**

Arjun's gut twisted as he pulled up Dr. Halloran's publicly available research. **She had authored dozens of papers on organ scarcity and ethics in transplantation.** Her public persona was a champion for reform, advocating for policy changes to reduce the waiting list for transplants. But here, in the Broker's documents, she was listed as a key facilitator—**not just aware of the black market, but actively involved in its logistics.**

Hospitals in on the Game

The more Arjun investigated, the more disturbing patterns emerged. **Several hospitals in different countries were listed in the network's files, not as victims of theft but as collaborators.** Some were smaller private clinics where regulations were easily circumvented. Others were prestigious institutions, the kind that boasted of advanced technology and world-class care.

These hospitals were not just blind participants; they were **beneficiaries.** The records showed that certain transplant

THE ORGAN BROKER

procedures were billed under fake patient names, with medical directors signing off on surgeries they knew were illegal. **The network's reach extended into hospital boards, allowing them to bypass scrutiny by regulators.**

Some of the documents pointed toward **kickbacks paid to administrators, hush money to cover illegal transplants, and even fake death certificates issued to donors who "disappeared" after giving up their organs.**

The Government's Hand

As the pieces came together, Arjun discovered something even more alarming—**government officials were complicit.** His search through public records revealed that several high-ranking politicians had received transplants at suspiciously short notice. **Their names matched the network's records, hidden under aliases and protected by layers of secrecy.**

But the evidence didn't stop at individual politicians. **There were entire departments—particularly immigration offices and public health sectors—that appeared to be turning a blind eye to the trafficking.** Some officials were even listed as recipients of bribes in exchange for speeding up patient transfers or issuing medical visas for "donors" flown in from other countries.

Refugee camps and migrant detention centers were hotbeds for this trafficking network. Desperate people without documentation were taken from these places, with government officials either paid to look the other way or actively helping to funnel victims into the black market pipeline. **In exchange, those officials received payouts or promises of medical treatment abroad.**

Arjun's hands shook as he stared at the documents in front of him. **How far did this corruption go?** How could an entire system built on trust and healing be complicit in such horrors?

Doctors with Two Faces

The most devastating revelation came when Arjun dug deeper into the roles played by other doctors in the network. **Some of the most respected figures in medicine were on the payroll.** Surgeons who had once been mentors and peers were listed in the files—people he had admired, who had inspired him to become a doctor in the first place.

They wore two faces—**publicly championing ethical medicine while quietly profiting from the sale of human organs.** They hosted charity events, published articles on medical ethics, and appeared at international conferences as experts. But behind closed doors, they facilitated illegal transplants, arranged for the transport of donors, and pocketed massive fees for their services.

One surgeon in particular caught Arjun's attention—**Dr. Vishal Mehta**, the head of a renowned transplant unit in Mumbai. **Arjun had once looked up to Mehta as a mentor, a pioneer in heart surgery.** But now, his name was linked to dozens of illegal operations, and his clinic appeared in multiple entries on the Broker's spreadsheet.

The betrayal cut deeper than any scalpel ever could. Arjun felt sick to his stomach. **These were not nameless criminals operating in the shadows—these were people he had trusted, people who had sworn the same oath as him.** They had shattered that oath without hesitation, all for the sake of power and profit.

THE ORGAN BROKER

A Global Conspiracy

It became clear that this wasn't just an underground operation—it was **a global conspiracy, with players at every level of the medical and political system.** The network spanned continents, linking corrupt doctors, hospital administrators, government officials, and wealthy clients into a seamless operation. **Each part of the machine relied on the others—politicians ensuring protection, doctors performing the surgeries, and hospitals covering the paperwork.**

And at the center of it all was the Broker—a faceless puppet master pulling the strings, ensuring that every organ, every surgery, and every bribe was perfectly coordinated. **The Broker wasn't just a middleman—he was the architect of an empire built on human bodies.**

The Cost of the Truth

Arjun sat in silence, overwhelmed by the weight of what he had uncovered. **The truth was worse than he had imagined.** It wasn't just about saving his son—it was about dismantling a system that thrived on the suffering of the powerless.

He knew now that there was no way out—not for him, not for Aarav. **The network was too powerful, its roots too deep.** Even if he exposed the truth, the people involved would bury the evidence, eliminate the witnesses, and continue their work without missing a beat.

And if he tried to walk away? **They would take everything from him—his career, his freedom, and his son's life.**

The Decision

Arjun stared at the documents spread across his desk, his mind racing. **He had a choice to make, but it was no choice at all.** If he stayed silent, he would be complicit in the deaths of countless others—**refugees, prisoners, children whose lives would be stolen for the benefit of the rich and powerful.** But if he spoke out, the network would destroy him—and Aarav would pay the ultimate price.

The weight of the decision pressed down on him, suffocating him. **He was trapped in a web of lies and betrayal, with no way out that wouldn't leave him broken.**

In the end, the only thing Arjun knew for certain was this: **the masks were shattered, and he could never see the world the same way again.** Every patient, every colleague, every politician—it was all a performance, a carefully constructed illusion to hide the rot that lay beneath.

And Arjun, despite his best intentions, was now part of it.

Chapter 12: Organ Farm

The plane flew low over the ocean, its engines humming steadily against the roar of the wind. Arjun sat by the window, staring blankly at the rolling waves below. His heart pounded with dread. **He was being taken to a place that no one was supposed to know about—a place that existed beyond the reach of laws, morality, or even humanity.**

For weeks now, he had been following the threads of the conspiracy, uncovering layer after layer of corruption. What he thought was just a black-market organ trade had revealed itself to be something far more sinister—**a global operation with ties to governments, hospitals, and corporate interests.** But the most horrifying discovery was still ahead of him: the **Organ Farm.**

This was the Broker's trump card, the heart of the operation. **A secret offshore facility where victims were kept alive for the sole purpose of harvesting their organs, piece by piece.** And now, Arjun was on his way there. He had been summoned, told that the final payment for his son's heart was a visit to this facility.

It wasn't just a demand—it was a threat. **The Broker wanted to show him what lay beneath the surface of the** operation, to make sure he understood the consequences of betrayal.

The Island of No Return

The plane touched down on a narrow runway, the island looming ahead, dark and unwelcoming. There was no airport terminal, no customs office—just a series of makeshift buildings surrounded by high fences topped with barbed wire. **It looked more like a prison than a medical facility.**

A man in a dark suit greeted Arjun at the bottom of the stairs, his face impassive. "Dr. Malhotra," he said with a nod. "Welcome to the farm."

The way he said it made Arjun's stomach turn. **This place wasn't just a metaphorical farm—it was a literal one.** Human bodies, treated like livestock, grown and harvested for their organs whenever the market demanded it.

Arjun followed the man in silence, his heart heavy with dread. **He had seen horrors in the operating rooms of the black-market clinics, but this—this was something else.**

The Facility

Inside the main building, the smell of antiseptic was overwhelming, masking the deeper, more pungent stench of fear and decay. **Rows of beds stretched out as far as the eye could see, each one occupied by a patient in various stages of sedation.**

Some were hooked up to IVs, their bodies frail and skeletal, kept alive just enough to preserve the organs within. Others looked healthier—recent arrivals, no doubt, awaiting their first "extraction." The staff moved between the beds with cold

THE ORGAN BROKER

efficiency, adjusting monitors, administering drugs, and making notes on clipboards.

"These are our donors," the man explained, his voice as emotionless as the staff around him. "We keep them here until their organs are needed. Some last for years, others... not so long."

Arjun's mind reeled. **These weren't donors—they were prisoners. Slaves.** Kept alive in a twilight state, their bodies picked apart, organ by organ, until there was nothing left. He scanned the room, his eyes searching for any sign of humanity, any glimmer of hope in the deadened faces around him. **There was none.**

"Why did you bring me here?" Arjun asked, his voice barely above a whisper.

"To show you the cost of your choices," the man replied. "You've benefited from this system. Your son is alive because of it. Now, you need to understand what that really means."

The Truth

They led him deeper into the facility, past rooms where organs were harvested and stored in sterile containers, waiting to be shipped to the highest bidder. **The cold, clinical efficiency of it all made Arjun sick to his core.** This was a system that ran on blood and flesh, reducing human beings to nothing more than spare parts.

In one room, Arjun saw a young girl—no older than twelve—lying unconscious on a gurney, her chest already marked for surgery. **Her body was perfectly healthy, but that wouldn't matter for long.** Soon, her organs would be removed, one by one, until there was nothing left to take.

The man noticed Arjun's horrified expression. "She'll go to a good cause," he said with a shrug. "Some billionaire in Dubai is paying top dollar for her liver. His daughter has a rare genetic disorder—this is her only chance."

"And her chance?" Arjun snapped, his voice shaking with fury. "What about her life?"

The man looked at him, surprised by the outburst. "She's a street kid, Doctor. No one's coming for her. Better her organs save someone who matters."

The words hit Arjun like a punch to the gut. He had been telling himself the same thing for months—justifying his actions by convincing himself that the people he took organs from were better off dead, that their lives didn't matter in the grand scheme of things.

But standing here, seeing the faces of the victims up close, he couldn't lie to himself any longer. **These people weren't statistics or anonymous bodies—they were human beings, with lives, families, and futures that had been stolen from them.**

The Choice

As they continued through the facility, Arjun felt a growing sense of unease. **The Broker's message was clear: You're one of us now.** There was no turning back, no way out. **If he tried to expose the truth, they would come for him—and for Aarav.** The thought of his son, lying helpless in a hospital bed, vulnerable to the Broker's wrath, terrified him more than anything.

Finally, they reached the heart of the operation—a secure room where the most valuable organs were stored. Arjun was

THE ORGAN BROKER

led to a glass case, inside which a human heart floated in a preservation solution.

"That's your son's next heart," the man said, his voice casual. "When the time comes, we'll have it ready. All you have to do is keep playing along."

Arjun stared at the heart, bile rising in his throat. This was it—the final nail in his coffin. **They owned him now.** If he wanted to keep Aarav alive, he would have to continue doing their bidding. There was no escape, no way to redeem himself.

But there was one thing he could still do—**he could expose the truth.**

The Decision

Arjun's mind raced. **He could walk out of here, return to his life, and pretend none of this had ever happened.** He could continue performing surgeries, continue taking organs from the innocent and the vulnerable, all to keep his son alive.

Or he could bring it all down. **He could gather evidence, expose the conspiracy to the world, and destroy the Broker's empire once and for all.**

But doing so would come at a terrible cost. **If he exposed the truth, they would kill him—and Aarav would die without the heart he so desperately needed.**

Arjun felt his hands shake as he weighed the decision. **Was his son's life worth all of this?** Could he live with himself knowing that he had sacrificed countless others to save Aarav?

He looked at the heart floating in the glass case, his vision blurring with tears. **He was trapped.** No matter what choice he made, someone would suffer.

The Breaking Point

As the man led him back toward the exit, Arjun's mind whirled with possibilities. **How could he bring down a system so vast, so entrenched in power and corruption?** He was just one man, a surgeon who had already betrayed his oath to save his son. **But maybe that betrayal could be turned into something else.**

If he gathered enough evidence—documents, names, records—**he could blow the whistle, send everything to the media, and let the world see the truth.** It wouldn't be easy, and it would certainly cost him his life. But maybe, just maybe, it would be enough to dismantle the system. **Maybe it would be enough to save future lives.**

As they approached the plane that would take him back to the mainland, Arjun made his decision.

He would fight back.

Chapter 13: Chasing Redemption

Arjun's heart pounded as he stared at the covert recorder hidden in the lining of his jacket. **It was a small, insignificant-looking device, but it could bring down an empire.** The organ trafficking ring was too powerful to dismantle with a single action—he needed to be careful, to document everything. This was his only way to bring justice to the countless lives stolen and sold by the network.

He knew the risks. **If the Broker discovered what he was doing, it wouldn't just cost Arjun his life—it would cost Aarav's life too.** The thought of his son lying helpless in the hospital bed haunted him, but it also gave him purpose. **If he didn't stop this, the cycle would continue.** More people would be abducted, coerced, and harvested, their lives extinguished to sustain the rich and powerful. He couldn't live with that burden any longer.

The First Recording

It began during one of the regular meetings with the Broker's associates. **Arjun kept his face neutral, his voice steady, even as his hands shook under the table.** His recorder, sewn carefully into his jacket, captured every word.

The meeting was chilling in its casual efficiency. They discussed logistics, transport routes, and quotas for the next batch of donors, as if they were moving cargo instead of human beings.

"We need six kidneys, two hearts, and a liver by the end of the month," one of the men said, tapping a pen against his notepad. "We'll pull from the refugee camps—less paperwork that way."

Arjun swallowed his disgust, forcing himself to nod. **Every conversation was evidence, every detail a nail in the network's coffin.**

As the meeting went on, he learned horrifying new truths. **The organ farm wasn't the only facility; there were others—more hidden clinics scattered across the globe, each one feeding the insatiable demand for transplants.** The network was vast, tangled in a web of bribes, blackmail, and political protection.

In Too Deep

Recording the meetings was only the first step. **Arjun needed more—patient records, financial documents, anything that could tie the operation to the powerful people behind it.** He began sneaking into restricted areas, using his knowledge of hospital systems to access confidential files. It was a dangerous game—one mistake, and everything would come crashing down.

The tension gnawed at him day and night. **He lived in constant fear of being discovered, every glance over his shoulder a reminder of how close he was to the edge.** But the more he uncovered, the more determined he became. **This** wasn't just about redemption—it was about doing what was right.

One night, he found what he had been searching for: **a series of encrypted financial transactions linking the organ farm to a network of offshore accounts.** The documents detailed bribes paid to government officials, payments to surgeons, and transfers to hospitals across several countries. **It was irrefutable proof that the conspiracy reached the highest levels of power.**

The Betrayal

Arjun thought he was being careful, but in a world as dangerous as this, there was no such thing as safety. **One of the network's operatives—a low-level courier—grew suspicious of Arjun's actions.** It wasn't long before the Broker found out.

Arjun's phone buzzed late one night with a message from the Broker: **"We know."**

The blood drained from Arjun's face. **He had been exposed.** Panic surged through him, but there was no time to waste. He grabbed his files, the recordings, and his laptop, shoving everything into a bag. **He needed to disappear—now.**

He knew the Broker wouldn't hesitate to send people after him. **The network had eyes everywhere, and they wouldn't stop until they silenced him.**

The Chase Begins

Arjun left his home under the cover of darkness, his heart racing. **Every shadow felt like a threat, every passing car a potential enemy.** He had to move fast—if he stayed in one place for too long, they would find him.

Using burner phones and fake IDs, Arjun made his way to a safehouse provided by a journalist contact—**the only person he trusted to help him expose the truth.** The journalist, an investigative reporter named Maya, had been following whispers of the organ trafficking ring for years but had never been able to gather enough evidence to blow the story open.

"This is it," Maya said, her eyes wide as she looked over the files Arjun had brought. "This is everything we need to take them down."

But Arjun wasn't so sure. **The network was powerful, and they would do whatever it took to protect themselves.** "We need to be careful," he warned. "If they find out where we are, it's over."

Maya nodded grimly. "I know. But this story needs to come out."

Hunted

The safehouse didn't stay safe for long. **The Broker's men tracked Arjun down, forcing him and Maya to flee in the dead of night.** They moved from city to city, never staying in one place for more than a few days.

Everywhere they went, the danger followed. **Anonymous messages threatened Arjun's family, warning him to stop.** The Broker's reach extended further than Arjun had imagined—**even the police couldn't be trusted.**

But despite the danger, Arjun refused to back down. **He had come too far to turn back now.** He had sacrificed too much, crossed too many lines. **If he was going to survive this, if Aarav was going to have a future, the truth had to come out.**

The Final Push

In a desperate move, Arjun and Maya contacted an international human rights organization. With their help, they arranged to leak the documents to the media, ensuring that the story would go public before the network could silence them. **It was a gamble—a dangerous one—but it was their only chance.**

As the clock ticked down to the release, the pressure mounted. **The Broker's men were closing in, and time was running out.** Every second felt like an eternity, every moment a reminder that one mistake could cost them everything.

On the night of the release, Arjun sat in front of his laptop, his hands shaking as he uploaded the final files. **It was done.** The truth was out—there was no going back.

A Reckoning

The story hit the news like a thunderclap, sending shockwaves through the medical community and beyond. **Hospitals were raided, officials were arrested, and the network's operations were dismantled piece by piece.**

But the victory came at a cost. **The Broker disappeared, vanishing into the shadows, his empire shattered but not destroyed.** And though the media celebrated the exposure of the organ trafficking ring, Arjun knew the fight was far from over. **The people behind the network were still out there—waiting, watching, planning their next move.**

The Price of Redemption

In the aftermath, Arjun returned to the hospital, exhausted but relieved. **He had done the right thing—but at what cost?**

His life was forever changed, and the weight of his actions would haunt him for the rest of his days.

As he stood by Aarav's bedside, watching his son sleep peacefully, he knew that the journey wasn't over. **Redemption wasn't a destination—it was a path, one that he would have to walk for the rest of his life.**

But for the first time in months, Arjun felt a flicker of hope. **He had faced the darkness—and survived.**

Chapter 14: The Scalpel's Edge

The clinic was nothing more than an abandoned building, hastily converted into a makeshift operating room. **Broken windows let in the damp night air, and the flicker of a dim lamp cast erratic shadows on the stained walls.** Arjun Malhotra stood in the center of the chaos, his heart hammering against his ribs, his hands cold despite the humid air.

His son, Aarav, lay unconscious on a gurney in front of him, his chest rising and falling unevenly. The heart—the stolen heart that had kept him alive for months—was failing. Arjun had known this day would come, but not like this. Not here, in this crumbling ruin, surrounded by danger on all sides.

He had brought everything he could: scalpels, syringes, sutures, tubes, and the new heart—the one the Broker had promised and threatened to take away if Arjun ever crossed him. But now, **the world was closing in from every direction.**

The traffickers were coming for him, furious at his betrayal. The authorities were closing in too, following the breadcrumbs he had scattered to expose the black-market organ trade. And here he was, at the edge of it all, with only one mission: to save Aarav.

No Time Left

Arjun took a deep breath, willing his hands to stop trembling. **He had performed hundreds of surgeries under pressure, but none of them felt as impossible as this.**

Every sound outside the clinic made his heart skip a beat. **Any moment now, they could burst through the door—either the traffickers demanding their organ back, or the police ready to arrest him for everything he had done.** There was no time to wait for help. **If he didn't replace Aarav's heart now, his son would die.**

He looked down at Aarav's fragile form, the child he had sacrificed everything for. **This was the boy he had lied for, killed for, betrayed his oath for.** And now, here they were—father and son—on the edge of life and death, with only Arjun's hands standing between them and the abyss.

A Broken Oath

As Arjun prepped for the surgery, a thousand thoughts raced through his mind. **He thought of the promises he had made—both to himself and to the people whose lives he had destroyed to get here.**

The image of the boy—the one whose heart now beat weakly inside Aarav—flashed in his mind. **The refugees, the prisoners, the children trafficked for their organs.** Their faces haunted him, but he pushed them away. **This wasn't the time to reflect. This was the time to act.**

He knew that this surgery wasn't just about saving Aarav's life—it was about everything he had done to get here. **The scalpel in his hand was more than a tool—it was a symbol** of every compromise, every sin, and every betrayal that had led him to this moment.

The Operation Begins

Arjun worked quickly, every movement precise despite the chaos around him. **He knew the procedure by heart—cut, clamp, suture, repeat.** But this time was different. **This was his son.** Every incision felt personal, every drop of blood a reminder of what was at stake.

He sliced into Aarav's chest, exposing the failing heart beneath. **It was like holding time in his hands—fragile, fleeting, impossible to control.** The heart had served its purpose, but now it was giving out, and Arjun needed to replace it with the new one.

He reached into the cooler, pulling out the donor heart. **It was still warm, beating faintly inside the preservation fluid.** He placed it carefully onto the tray, his hands steady, his mind sharp. **This was it—the moment that would decide everything.**

An Unwelcome Visitor

The door to the clinic creaked open, and Arjun froze, the scalpel still in his hand. **His worst fears had come true.**

A man stepped inside, his silhouette sharp against the dim light. **It was the Broker.** His expression was unreadable, but the glint in his eyes told Arjun everything he needed to know—**he wasn't here to help.**

"You've made a mess of things, Doctor," the Broker said quietly, stepping closer to the operating table. "You thought you could expose us and walk away?"

Arjun's heart raced, but he kept his hands steady over Aarav's chest. "If you're here to stop me, you're too late. I'm finishing this."

The Broker smiled—a slow, cold smile that didn't reach his eyes. "I'm not here to stop you. I just wanted to see if you had it in you."

Arjun clenched his jaw, refusing to rise to the bait. **He didn't have time for games.** Every second counted. **Aarav's life was slipping away, and Arjun couldn't afford any distractions.**

The Final Cut

Ignoring the Broker, Arjun returned to the surgery. **He worked quickly but carefully, replacing the failing heart with the new one.** Every stitch, every clamp, every suture was a race against time. **His hands moved with the precision of a man who had spent his entire life preparing for this moment.**

But the weight of everything—**the lies, the betrayals, the stolen lives—pressed down on him like a vice.** He could feel the ghosts of the people he had harmed watching him, waiting to see if he would make it right.

With one final cut, Arjun completed the transplant. **The new heart was in place, beating steadily inside Aarav's chest.** For a moment, Arjun felt a wave of relief wash over him. **He had done it. Aarav was alive.**

A Choice and a Consequence

Arjun stepped back from the operating table, his hands slick with blood. **The surgery was over, but the nightmare**

wasn't. The Broker was still there, watching him with an amused expression.

"You know this doesn't change anything," the Broker said. "You're still one of us, Doctor. No matter what you do, you'll never escape."

Arjun stared at him, his heart pounding in his chest. **He knew the Broker was right.** He had crossed too many lines, made too many compromises. **Even if Aarav lived, Arjun's soul was stained with the things he had done.**

But as he looked down at his son—**alive, breathing, safe**—Arjun knew that some things were worth the cost. He had saved his child. **And that was all that mattered.**

The Escape

The sound of sirens echoed in the distance, growing louder with each passing second. **The authorities were coming.**

The Broker glanced toward the door, a flicker of annoyance crossing his face. "Looks like you're out of time, Doctor."

Arjun didn't hesitate. **He grabbed Aarav, wrapping him in a blanket, and bolted toward the back door.** The police would arrest him if they caught him—and the network would kill him if he stayed. **There was no time to think, only time to run.**

He burst out into the night, his son cradled in his arms, and ran toward the waiting car Maya had arranged for him. **The headlights flicked on, and the engine roared to life.**

"Get in!" Maya shouted, throwing open the passenger door.

Arjun climbed in, clutching Aarav close, and the car sped off into the darkness. **The clinic disappeared behind them, swallowed by the night.**

The Road Ahead

As the car raced down the empty road, Arjun felt a strange sense of peace settle over him. **He had done what he set out to do—he had saved his son.**

But he knew that the road ahead wouldn't be easy. **The authorities would hunt him. The network would come for him.** There would be no peace, no safety. **Only the promise of more battles to fight, more sacrifices to make.**

But as Aarav stirred in his arms, his tiny heart beating steadily against Arjun's chest, **he knew it had all been worth it.** He would face whatever came next—**the arrests, the betrayals, the dangers—because some things were worth everything.**

He kissed the top of Aarav's head, a tear slipping down his cheek. **"We'll be okay,"** he whispered. **"We'll find a way."**

And for the first time in a long time, **Arjun believed it.**

Chapter 15: The Final Trade

The desert sun blazed mercilessly overhead, casting long shadows across the cracked earth. Arjun Malhotra stood at the edge of the airstrip, his heart pounding in his chest as he cradled his son, Aarav, against him. The plane in front of him—a small private jet—hummed with anticipation, its door yawning open, promising escape. But **this was no ordinary departure.**

This was a crossroads—a moment that would decide everything. **The truth or Aarav.** Justice or freedom. **One could live, but the other would die.**

Arjun had spent the last few weeks running—evading traffickers, the police, and the ghosts of his own sins. **He had gathered enough evidence to dismantle the organ trafficking empire**, to expose the network of corrupt doctors, politicians, and criminals who profited from stolen lives.

But **the truth came at a cost**—and that cost was hanging over him now, heavy as a noose tightening around his neck.

A Devil's Bargain

The Broker had given Arjun an impossible choice. **If Arjun wanted to escape with his son**, he had to bury the evidence. **Walk away. Delete the files.** Never speak of what he knew.

If he tried to expose the truth, **Aarav's heart would stop.** The network's reach was vast, and the new heart that kept Aarav alive—**a heart they had stolen, traded, and implanted under their watchful eye**—came with conditions.

They could stop it with a single command. **A remote signal, they said. A heartbeat switch, embedded inside the pacemaker connected to Aarav's heart.** They would shut it down if Arjun betrayed them.

He had heard their threat on the phone that morning:

"We own you, Doctor. Your son lives because we allow it. Bury the files. Board the plane. Or bury your boy."

The Weight of the Truth

Arjun looked down at Aarav, his son's small hand gripping his sleeve even as he slept. **The boy's face was peaceful, unaware of the war raging around him.** Arjun had fought tooth and nail to get him here—to this moment of escape. **But now, with freedom so close, the cost felt unbearable.**

He thought of the victims—**the refugees taken from camps, the prisoners forced to sell their organs, the children abducted off the streets.** He thought of the countless lives destroyed by the organ trade, reduced to numbers in a ledger. **He carried their ghosts with him, as much a part of him now as the scalpel in his hand.**

Arjun had the evidence. **If he released it, the network would fall.** Hospitals would be raided, politicians arrested, and doctors stripped of their licenses. **Justice would finally be served.**

But justice wouldn't save Aarav. **If he hit send on the files, his son would die.**

Maya's Plea

"Don't do this, Arjun."

Maya's voice pulled him back from the edge of his thoughts. **The journalist had risked everything to help him gather the evidence**, to bring the story to light. She stood beside him now, her expression filled with anguish.

"You can't let them win," she whispered. "You can't let all those people die in silence."

"I know," Arjun whispered, the words choking in his throat. "But Aarav... if I send the files, they'll kill him."

Maya's eyes shimmered with unshed tears. "If you walk away, they'll keep killing. How many more children will they take? How many more lives will they destroy?"

The weight of her words crushed him. Arjun knew she was right. **But knowing didn't make the choice any easier.**

A Father's Dilemma

Arjun paced along the edge of the airstrip, the phone in his hand a lifeline and a curse. **On the screen was the file—thousands of documents, recordings, and testimonies that could dismantle the organ trafficking network for good.**

All he had to do was press send.

But pressing send would kill Aarav.

Arjun's heart wrenched in his chest. **He was a doctor, a man sworn to save lives.** But he was also a father. And no father could be expected to sacrifice his own child. **Could he?**

The wind whipped across the airstrip, stinging his eyes and blurring his vision. **There was no right answer—only loss.**

A Deal with the Devil

His phone buzzed. Another message from the Broker:

"Last chance, Doctor. Board the plane. Delete the files. Or we stop the heart."

Arjun stared at the words, bile rising in his throat. **It was a simple choice. Life or truth.** He had made impossible decisions before—**cutting into bodies, deciding which patients lived and which ones didn't.** But none of those choices compared to this.

The phone felt heavy in his hand. **The fate of hundreds—maybe thousands—of innocent people rested on the decision he would make in the next few moments.**

But so did his son's life.

The Final Trade

Arjun knelt beside Aarav's sleeping form, brushing a strand of hair from the boy's forehead. **His son's heart beat steadily beneath his small chest—a stolen heart, a borrowed life.**

"I love you, beta," Arjun whispered, his voice breaking. **"I hope one day you'll understand."**

With trembling fingers, **he unlocked his phone.** The cursor blinked on the screen, waiting for his command. **Delete or send.**

He glanced at Maya, her face filled with silent hope. **She didn't know what he was about to do.**

Arjun closed his eyes, tears slipping down his cheeks. **He had made his decision.**

A Message in the Dark

His thumb hovered over the screen. **Delete or send.** One click, and everything would change. **The plane was waiting. The Broker was waiting.**

And then, without another thought—**he pressed send.**

The files uploaded in seconds, flashing across encrypted servers, blasting the truth into the open. **The story was out. There was no taking it back.**

Maya gasped, her hand flying to her mouth. "Arjun..."

"I had to," Arjun whispered, his voice raw. "I had to."

The Heartbeat Stops

For a moment, there was silence. Then, a sound that shattered Arjun's world.

Aarav's heart monitor—**the steady, rhythmic beep that had been his lifeline—stopped.**

Flatline.

Arjun's breath caught in his throat. "No—no, no, no!" He dropped the phone, grabbing his medical bag with frantic hands. **He had known this would happen—but he wasn't ready.**

"Aarav! Aarav, stay with me!" Arjun cried, tearing open his son's shirt, preparing for chest compressions. **His mind raced through the steps of CPR, but his hands shook so violently he could barely keep steady.**

Maya knelt beside him, her hands trembling. **"You can save him, Arjun. You have to."**

The Scalpel's Edge

Arjun's training kicked in, his emotions pushed to the side. **There was no time for fear, no time for regret—only the next move, the next chance.** He grabbed a syringe, injecting epinephrine into Aarav's chest. **He pressed his hands over his son's heart and began the compressions.**

"One, two, three—breathe!"

He tilted Aarav's head back, giving him mouth-to-mouth, then returned to the compressions. **The seconds stretched into eternity.**

But the heart monitor remained silent. **No pulse. No beat.**

"Come on, Aarav," Arjun whispered desperately. "**Come back to me.**"

The Miracle

For one agonizing moment, Arjun thought he had lost his son. **But then—**

Beep.

The monitor chirped once. Then again. **A heartbeat. Weak, but there.**

Arjun sagged with relief, tears streaming down his face. **He had done it.** Against all odds, **his son was alive.**

A New Beginning

The sound of sirens echoed in the distance—**the authorities were coming.**

Maya touched Arjun's shoulder, her voice gentle. "**We have to go.**"

Arjun nodded, scooping Aarav into his arms. **The truth was out, and they were free.** But the road ahead would not be easy. **They would be hunted, hated by those who wanted to keep the secret buried.**

But Arjun didn't care. **He had saved his son. And he had done the right thing.**

For the first time in months, **he felt whole.**

Chapter 16: After the Harvest

The sun rose slowly over the distant hills, casting long shadows across the quiet hospital room. **Arjun Malhotra sat beside Aarav's bed**, exhausted beyond words. The rhythmic beep of the heart monitor was the only sound in the room—each beat a reminder that his son was alive. **Alive, but at a cost.**

The chaos of the past weeks felt like a blur—a nightmare stitched together from stolen organs, covert operations, and impossible choices. **He had exposed the truth. The organ trafficking ring was dismantled, its leaders either arrested or on the run.** The evidence he had leaked had sparked an international scandal, leaving governments scrambling to deny involvement and hospitals issuing hollow statements of condemnation.

But the victory felt hollow. **Aarav was alive, but so many others were not.** The faces of those he could not save haunted him, hovering in the back of his mind like ghosts that refused to be laid to rest. **He had won the battle, but at what cost?**

Lives Saved, Lives Lost

In the aftermath of the organ trade's collapse, the world celebrated the takedown of a powerful criminal network. **The media praised Arjun as a hero**, though his name was kept out of official reports to protect him from retaliation. But the cost of that victory was measured in more than headlines.

Some lives had been saved—**refugees, prisoners, and children who would have otherwise been harvested for parts.** But not all of them had made it. **Many of the victims had already been dismantled by the time the authorities arrived.** Some had died on the operating table, their lives extinguished to meet quotas and deadlines. Others had disappeared altogether, vanishing into the void created by the chaos.

The organ farm was shut down, but it was too late for so many. And for every donor who was freed, there were countless others who would never come home. **Their faces stayed with Arjun, lingering in the quiet moments between breaths, reminders of the price of survival.**

The Price of Truth

Arjun had thought that exposing the truth would bring him peace. **But peace proved to be as elusive as the future he had once dreamed of.** Every headline about the organ trade's downfall felt like a knife in his heart. **He had done the right thing, but that didn't make it any easier.**

His actions had come at a steep cost. **The people he had exposed were powerful, and their reach extended far beyond the courtroom.** Even with the network dismantled, Arjun knew that there were still those who wanted revenge. **He and Aarav would never be truly safe.**

Maya had warned him about the risks. "The truth doesn't set you free, Arjun. It just gives you a different kind of cage."

And she was right. Arjun and Aarav were alive, but they were living in the shadows—**moving from one safehouse to another, constantly looking over their shoulders.** The danger wasn't over, not by a long shot.

Broken Promises

Arjun stared down at his hands—the same hands that had saved countless lives, but had also taken part in unspeakable horrors. **He had broken every promise he had made to himself**, every vow he had taken when he became a doctor. **He had sworn to heal, to do no harm. Instead, he had stolen organs, betrayed innocent people, and played god with human lives.**

Was there any redemption for someone like him? **Or were some wounds too deep to heal?**

Every life he had saved felt like a reminder of the lives he couldn't. **For every child he had rescued, another had died on an operating table.** For every refugee spared, another had vanished into the network, their organs sold to the highest bidder.

He had won, but victory had never felt so empty.

A Father's Guilt

Aarav stirred in his sleep, his small hand clutching the blanket draped over his body. **The scar on his chest was a stark reminder of the heart that beat beneath it—a heart stolen from another child.** Arjun's heart ached with guilt every time he looked at that scar. **He had saved his son, but at what cost?**

Would Aarav ever understand what his father had done to keep him alive? **Could Arjun ever forgive himself?**

He leaned forward, pressing a kiss to Aarav's forehead. **"I'm sorry,"** he whispered, though the words felt inadequate. **"I hope you'll understand one day."**

The Search for Redemption

In the weeks following the takedown of the network, **Arjun found himself searching for redemption in the only way he knew how—by continuing to save lives.** He volunteered at refugee clinics, working long hours in overcrowded hospitals where resources were scarce and patients endless.

But even in those moments of healing, the guilt followed him. No matter how many lives he saved, he couldn't escape the memories of those he had lost. **The ghosts of the past were always there, lurking in the shadows, whispering reminders of his sins.**

He had thought that saving Aarav would make everything worth it. **But now, he wasn't so sure.**

The Road Ahead

One night, after another long shift at the clinic, Arjun sat on the porch of his latest safehouse, watching the stars. **The world felt vast and indifferent, a reminder that life went on, even after everything he had been through.**

Maya joined him, sitting beside him in silence. **They had become unlikely allies—partners in survival, bonded by shared trauma and the knowledge of what they had lost.**

"Do you think it was worth it?" Arjun asked quietly, his voice barely audible over the sound of the wind.

Maya didn't answer right away. **She had lost people too—friends, sources, colleagues—casualties of the truth they had fought to expose.**

"Sometimes," she said at last. "And sometimes not. But we did what we had to do."

Arjun nodded, though the weight in his chest remained. He knew that the road ahead would be long and uncertain. **There would be more challenges, more battles to fight, more ghosts to confront.**

But for the first time in a long time, **he felt something resembling hope.** He didn't know if redemption was possible. **But he was willing to try.**

A Father's Promise

As the night deepened, Arjun went back inside and knelt beside Aarav's bed. **He stroked his son's hair, his heart aching with love and guilt and hope all at once.**

"I don't know if I'll ever make this right," he whispered. "But I'll keep trying. For you."

And in that moment, **he made a promise—to Aarav, to the people he had lost, and to himself.** He would keep going, no matter how hard it got. **He would keep fighting, keep healing, and keep searching for a way to make peace with the past.**

Because **after the harvest, there was still life to be lived.** And for now, that was enough.

Thank You for Reading

DEAR READER,

Thank you for embarking on this journey with **The Doctor's Dilemma Collection**. I truly appreciate your time, curiosity, and support in exploring the intricate world of medicine through these stories. If this book resonated with you or inspired new perspectives, please consider supporting future projects and publications. Your generous contributions make it possible to continue creating meaningful content.

Support My Work:

Venmo: @Nileshlp

Cash App: $drnileshlp

BTC

bc1qs72228z6pauw3rk9tej9f6umu4y9gz289y3cvn

ETH

0xE1DAE6F656c900a4b24257b587ac0856E1e346D2

Every bit of support goes a long way in sustaining my passion for storytelling and public health advocacy. Once again, thank you from the bottom of my heart. Your encouragement and generosity mean the world to me.

Warm regards,

Dr. Nilesh Panchal

Author and Public Health Practitioner

Don't miss out!

Visit the website below and you can sign up to receive emails whenever Dr. Nilesh Panchal publishes a new book. There's no charge and no obligation.

https://books2read.com/r/B-A-JKGNC-XJSDF

BOOKS 2 READ

Connecting independent readers to independent writers.

Did you love *The Organ Broker*? Then you should read *The Last Patient*[1] by Dr. Nilesh Panchal!

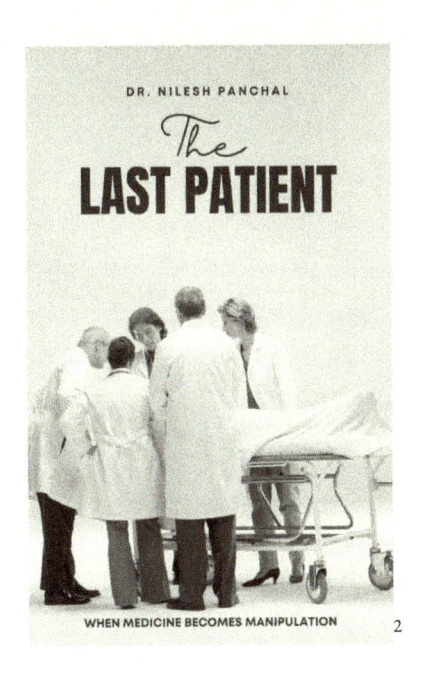

In ***The Last Patient***, Dr. Rahul Varma relocates to the quiet town of Hazelwood, hoping for a peaceful practice, only to uncover a chilling secret: the residents are unknowingly being used as subjects in a covert clinical trial for a new psychiatric drug. As he delves deeper, he unravels a web of deception involving the pharmaceutical company, town officials, and even some of his own patients. With mounting pressure to stay silent and his career on the line, Dr. Varma must decide whether to risk everything to expose the truth. Blending medical ethics,

---

1. https://books2read.com/u/3nPrr8

2. https://books2read.com/u/3nPrr8

small-town intrigue, and psychological suspense, *The Last Patient* is a gripping exploration of the dark side of clinical research and the moral cost of justice.

Read more at https://drmedhealth.com/.

Also by Dr. Nilesh Panchal

Clinical Trials Mastery Series
Essentials of Clinical Trials
Clinical Trials: Ethical Considerations and Regulations
Clinical Trials Design and Methodology

Mastering the FDA Approval Process
Mastering New Drug Applications A Step-by-Step Guide
Navigating ANDA: Strategies for Effective Generic Drug Approval
Mastering PMA: A Comprehensive Guide to Premarket Approval for Medical Devices

The Doctor's Dilemma Collection
A Heartbeat Away
Human Trial
The Surgeon's Dilemma
The Last Patient
The Organ Broker

Standalone
Navigating FDA Drug Approval
Healthy Habits: A Kid's Guide to Wellness
Mastering Medical Terminology
Navigating the FDA 510(k) Process
Essential First Aid: Life-Saving Techniques for Everyone

Watch for more at https://drmedhealth.com/.

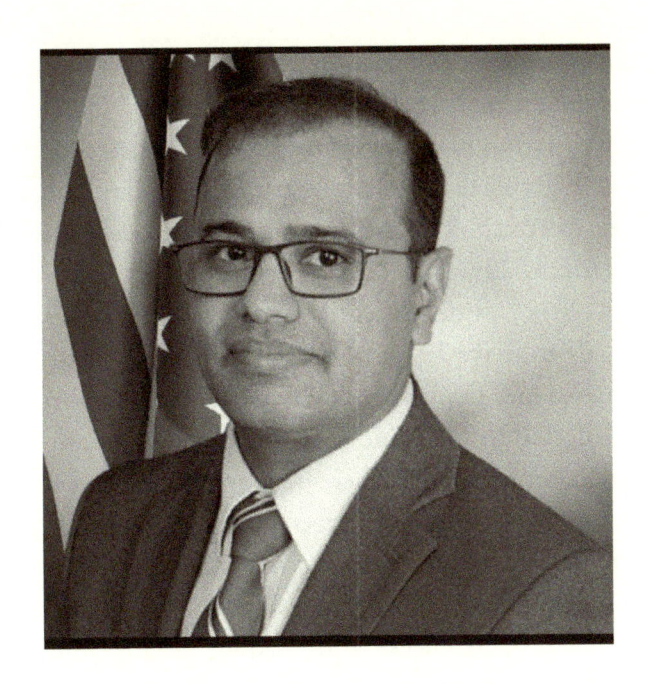

About the Author

Dr. Nilesh Panchal is a distinguished Public Health Practitioner and Health Scientist with over two decades of experience, making significant contributions to the fields of infectious diseases, mental health, and public health education. Holding a DrPH in Public Health Practice, Dr. Panchal is a prolific author known for his ability to translate complex medical concepts into accessible and engaging content for a broad audience. His work, including the acclaimed series "Global Outbreaks: The Saga of Humanity's Health Battles," provides invaluable insights into the challenges posed by infectious diseases, making it an authoritative source for understanding humanity's ongoing battle against deadly pathogens. Dr. Panchal's dedication to educating the public extends to his "Mindfulness and Well-Being Series," where his compassionate and practical approach empowers readers to enhance their mental and emotional well-being.

In addition to his focus on infectious diseases and mental health, Dr. Panchal has made remarkable strides in lifestyle medicine, particularly in the prevention of diabetes. His book series "Healthy Living, Healthy Future: Diabetes Prevention Series" offers evidence-based strategies that empower individuals to make lasting lifestyle changes for a healthier, diabetes-free life. Dr. Panchal's commitment to public health is also reflected in his guide "Essential First Aid: Life-Saving Techniques for Everyone," where he provides clear, step-by-step instructions for managing emergencies. Through his extensive research, Dr. Panchal continues to be a respected voice in global health, contributing to medical journals, speaking at international conferences, and leading health innovation projects aimed at integrating AI into clinical practice. His body of work not only informs but also inspires, making a lasting impact on global health practices and public education.

Read more at https://drmedhealth.com/.